MONKSBANE

BY

JACK FRERKER

PAX PUBLICATIONS — OLYMPIA, WASHINGTON

Published by PAX Publications, 7710 56th Avenue NE, Olympia WA

Copyright © 2007 by Jack Frerker. All rights reserved. No part of this book may be reproduced, stored in a retrieval system or transmitted, in any form or by any means, electronic, mechanical, photocopying, recording or otherwise, without the author's express written permission, except for short quotes or citations for purposes of literary critique or review.

Printed in the U S A, by Bang Printing of Brainerd MN

This is a work of fiction. All names, characters and incidents are from the author's imagination or used fictitiously. Reference to real persons is not intended and should not be inferred.

LIBRARY OF CONGRESS CATALOGING-IN-PUBLICATION DATA

Frerker, Jack, 1937 –
   MONKSBANE
   ISBN 978-0-9740080-4-2

ACKNOWLEDGMENTS

Thanks to the real monks of St. Martin's Abbey for the friendship and tolerance that they have shown me for over a decade. They bear but slight resemblance to their counterparts in my book.

Thanks also to the team of people who by now are integral to the publication of my books: Garn Turner for another inspired book cover; Richard Swanson for my website and all the other electronic wonders he works; and Paula Buckner, Tom Vickery and Joe Weir, without whose proofing and editing skills you loyal readers would almost certainly easily lose interest in my stories.

And, finally, my gratitude to the dedicated religious men and women around the globe who, without much fanfare, daily pray for us all and, it is to be hoped, do so without the intrusions of such fanciful things as I have dared to write about in this, my latest story. Blessings upon them all!

Jack Frerker

TO MY PARENTS AND GRANDPARENTS,

LOVINGLY AND GRATEFULLY

CHAPTER I

An electronic bell sounding throughout the monastery roused Father John Wintermann. He barely remembered having turned off his alarm clock some time earlier. Now, here he was about to miss Morning Prayer. He had no obligation to join the Benedictine monks at prayer, but his decision to pray the Hours of the Office with them had seemed right for a monastic retreat. *Not the best of beginnings, John!*

Studying with the Benedictines at St. Meinrad Seminary in southern Indiana had endeared him to their style of prayer, so the Abbey of St. Martin in metropolitan Olympia, Washington, seemed a logically suitable place for his retreat. Nestled amid huge Douglas firs on grounds adjacent to a university named for the abbey, it promised a reflective, prayerful setting, especially in the July absence of most students.

Having heard about the abbey from one of the priests of his diocese, and needing to recover his spiritual balance after the unsettling discovery of a skeleton outside Algoma and the equally unsettling events in the weeks thereafter, he chose it partly to avoid the miserable July heat of southern Illinois. Besides, he had never seen the beautiful Northwest. While it had taken most Algomans only a few weeks to restore calm to their lives after those fearsome events, Father John was hoping to finally recover his own equanimity on this retreat. And he was about to miss its first formal moment.

He dressed hurriedly and made his way down the corridor on the abbey's main floor. Turning left at its dead-end, he went through the door into the walkway to the church, only to be brought up short by the sight of Brother Robert sprawled on the floor a few yards ahead, his cane just beyond his outstretched hand.

Father John reached down to the monk and found him clearly unconscious, his pulse racing and his breathing labored. Father John decided to call 911 even before informing the monastic community, so he keyed in the number-code at the door he had just come through and went back to his room as quickly as his 64-year-old arthritic body would allow. After the phone call, he returned with a blanket, a pillow and the plastic bag that protected his suitcase against any leakage from his toiletries. It was to hold the bit of soil that he had noticed next to the monk.

He propped up the elderly man's head to make him as comfortable as he could before bagging the not-quite-muddy dirt and hurrying toward the church. By the time he emerged from the corridor's other end, the monks were just leaving the monastery church on their silent walk to breakfast.

The abbot was leading the exodus and, seeing Father John's harried look, came over to him at once. Father John quickly told him about Brother Robert, and the abbot immediately signaled to Brother Elwin. To the curious stares of the other monks, the three men hurried back down the winding corridor toward the still-motionless monk now lying beneath Father John's blanket.

While the abbot and Brother Elwin, a nurse, checked the old man, Father John moved the cane out of the way and noticed what looked like blood on its rubber tip.

"He may have a concussion," Brother Elwin was saying. "It's a good thing you've already called an ambulance, Father. Where'd you tell them to come?" He exuded competence, which had a calming influence on the two priests.

"I wasn't sure, so I suggested the church entrance," Father John responded. "I told them not to use their siren. I didn't think others needed to be alarmed." The abbot nodded in approval.

"Good," Brother Elwin said. "It's actually as close as they can get, with the monastery drive chained off, as it is. I'll wait for the paramedics at the main door of the church. They ought to be arriving any moment now." He rose and disappeared down the enclosed walkway.

Father John turned to the abbot. "I found some dirt beside him, and that's almost certainly blood on the rubber tip of his cane. He isn't bleeding, so it must belong to someone else. He could have hit an intruder on the face or head before being flattened. You may not want to alarm your monks, but I hope you investigate this thoroughly."

Abbot Mark studied Father John carefully. They had only met the previous evening upon Father John's arrival, but he had already taken a liking to the older priest. "I will, I promise you," he said. "After we're sure that Robert is off to the hospital, you can put that dirt and cane in my office for safekeeping, and we'll go over to breakfast. We'll have to hurry to make the 8 o'clock Mass. After that, I intend to visit Robert, and you're welcome to come along, if you like."

Within fifteen minutes they were walking into the monks' dining room in the main building of the school, and by 8:45, after the community Mass, the two were en route to nearby St. Peter's Hospital.

CHAPTER II

The abbot parked by the hospital's Emergency Room, and the two priests hurried inside. They learned at the nursing station that Brother Robert was still in the ER. "I want to anoint him," the abbot said in a calm but determined tone of voice.

He was shown into the bay where Brother Robert lay unconscious, and Father Julius from the abbey greeted him. "I thought you'd be coming, Abbot. I haven't anointed him yet, as I thought you'd want to yourself. Here are the oils. Come alone?"

"No. Father Wintermann's in the waiting room. He's making a retreat, remember? Where's Elwin?"

"Yes, I do remember. I'll go to him in the waiting room. Elwin's there also, I believe — or somewhere nearby. The doctor says it's probably a concussion but doesn't seem worried about Robert."

"I gathered as much from the nurse outside, that no one's that worried about his condition. Thanks for the oils. Come back as soon as you can to pray with me. And bring Elwin and Father Wintermann with you."

Father Julius was the hospital's chaplain and one of the older monks in the abbey. Like several other members of the monastic community, he held a position outside the monastery. Several were pastors nearby and one a chaplain at a hospital in Yakima on the other side of the Cascades. One was even at the tip of the Olympic Peninsula as chaplain to a small convent of cloistered nuns. Julius was the only of those men who lived at the monastery. All the other members of the small monastery — just under forty monks in total –

lived within its walls. Of those, a few taught at the university and several others held staff positions there — postmaster, librarian, campus minister. One was even foreman of the campus maintenance crew.

Father Julius soon returned with Brother Elwin and Father John in tow. They joined the abbot at the monk's bedside and joined in the prayers for the anointing. Brother Robert did not wake up while they were in the room and, at the conclusion of the rite, the abbot's glance at Brother Elwin prompted the younger monk to say: "It's all right. He'll come out of this okay."

As Abbot Mark handed the oils back to the chaplain, he said: "I think we'll leave him in your hands, Julius. Keep us posted, especially when he comes to. I want to ask him a few questions about how he fell. Father John and I will be returning to the monastery now. You need a ride, Elwin?"

"Yes. I came in the ambulance with Robert."

"Did you get breakfast?"

"No, but no big thing. I'll get something at our snack bar."

After the three priests again blessed Brother Robert, the abbot left for the monastery with his two passengers. "We'll be in plenty of time for Noon Prayer," he said to no one in particular while making his way to the abbey's car in the hospital parking lot.

CHAPTER III

At the abbey, Father John followed Abbot Mark into his office to retrieve the plastic bag with the clump of dirt from beside Brother Robert. He suggested that the cane remain there in case the bloodstain needed to be analyzed. "I'll try to puzzle out where this dirt came from. It might shed light on what happened to your monk," he said. The abbot nodded as his guest stepped out of his office.

What a way to begin my retreat, Father John mused as he went down the corridor to its dead end. *There's been precious little rest or reflection so far!* At the end of the long corridor, he turned and stepped through the door to scrutinize the floor immediately beyond for more traces of soil but found none. *It makes no sense that whoever accosted Brother Robert came from inside the monastery. But just in case that's what happened, let's think about how this might have gone down.*

If monastery security had been breached, there were only four entrances he knew of at which that might have happened, each with a number pad requiring a code to open the door. When he was given the proper numbers upon his arrival, he was told that the same code worked at each of those doors. Three of the doors entered the monastery proper; the fourth allowed entry only into the corridor to the church a few steps from where Brother Robert had fallen and from the door into the monastery's main corridor, the one Father John had come through when he discovered the fallen monk. Logically, whoever bumped into Brother Robert didn't come through that outer door because the un-coded church entrance just yards farther on could have brought him into the church and eventually to the place where the monk was found.

If there were a security breach, it had to be at the monastery door near where the monk fell, at the abbot's entrance at the other end of the main floor near the guest room Father John was occupying across from the abbot's office, or at the door to the monastery parking area one floor below.

Finding no more dirt where he was standing, he went back inside the monastery and carefully walked toward the stairwell. He searched the stairs carefully as he descended one story to the lowest floor of the monastery. Midway down the flight of stairs he found another clump of dirt that appeared to match his first sample. He picked it up carefully, placed it in the plastic bag beside the first piece and continued on to the monastery's bottom floor. The stairwell door opened out beside the coded door to the parking area for monastery vehicles, a story below the back of the monastery church. Seeing no dirt on the floor there, he turned left and went as far as the large monastery community room, several paces inside of which he saw another bit of soil. With that also safely inside the plastic bag, he paused to think.

I know of no other entrances to the cloister. Why would someone get into the monastery and come to this area ... unless ...

He looked up to survey the wall of glass patio doors in front of him. *Of course! Someone could have come through those doors!* A number of sliding panels lined the entire wall there, and he went to see if all were secured. The first one he came to — the one on the far left as he faced the wall of glass — was slightly ajar. Someone must not have locked it either that morning or the previous night.

Outside, a concrete slab extended the length of the room and went fifteen or so feet deep toward the east. Beyond that was an expanse of lawn that ended in a steep hill overlooking a meadow bordered on its left by a large forest of huge Douglas firs. The view from the patio was spectacular on a clear day. Mount Rainier rose majestically on the eastern horizon and looked so close that a stranger might think it only ten or twenty minutes away. Father John knew better, having been told the night before that it was more like two hours away by car.

He quickly determined that no easy access to that outside area lay to his right, so he turned left and carefully searched the grass on the north beyond the concrete patio. At the edge of the concrete, close to what he had been told was a small pond for goldfish, he found a narrow rut in the damp grass. The pieces of soil in his plastic bag looked like they could have come from there. The monastery parking area just beyond provided easy access to the rear of the monastery.

Father John looked closer at the rut and quickly realized that he was looking at a bicycle tire track. Last evening's brief rain had left the ground soggy enough to allow for such a track — and for muddy shoes, as well. This fifth access had to be where someone had invaded the cloister … but why?

He re-entered the monks' common room. Finding nothing after diligent scrutiny, he started to retrace his steps toward the second floor. Just before stepping outside the room, however, he noticed that the chess set on a table by the wall was missing the pawn just in front of the black queen. It was nowhere on the floor or nearby. He stored that for future consideration and made his way back upstairs to where the elderly monk had fallen.

He stood awhile in thought. *If someone came this way from below, he'd have had to leave his bicycle down there. And where in the world would he be heading? And for what reason?* He also realized that the bike was nowhere to be seen down below. *Given the several hours since the incident, there's been plenty of time to retrieve it.*

The only logical destination for the intruder had to be the church; the culprit could have easily gotten outside either through that other coded door a few steps away from the fallen monk or the glass door through which he had entered. *If all he wanted to do was steal a chess piece, why not leave the way he came in downstairs?* There had to be something else he wanted to do, and probably in the church. But the monks were in the church, surely, by the time he had gotten to where he literally ran into Brother Robert. It still didn't make sense to Father John, but he felt that he was making progress.

He made his way to the church and walked around, looking carefully for anything untoward. After a few minutes, he looked up to see the brother who served as sacristan step into the church. He continued his search but, moments later, there was a muffled cry from the small Eucharistic chapel: "What in heaven's name?"

As the young monk came out of the chapel, Father John asked: "What is it, Brother?"

"Some prankster in the community put a chess piece in front of the tabernacle. That isn't funny."

"You're right. It isn't. Let me take it back downstairs for you. You look busy. I'm heading back to the monastery, anyway," Father John said.

He headed back with the pawn but went directly to the abbot, instead of to the community room. The puzzle wasn't complete, but he believed that many of its pieces were in place.

It took only moments to relate what he knew, and the abbot, in turn, had something to tell him. "One of the young monks has the task of securing the glass doors in our recreation room each evening. He came to me all upset after I got back from St. Peter's. He had realized only moments earlier — to his great chagrin, as he said — that he had failed to secure one of those doors. He was feeling guilty, especially once he learned of Robert's fall.

"But now that I hear about that chess piece, I suspect there's more our young monk may wish to tell me. You see, he was a student here before joining us, and some of his friends are still taking classes here. This is beginning to sound like a student prank. Let me check with Robert. Once he's conscious, he may be able to shed some light on this."

A phone call to the hospital confirmed that the monk was indeed now able to speak, and the resultant conversation — brief, in deference to the monk's condition — apparently gave the abbot what he wanted.

"Just as I suspected! Robert said a student had burst through the door behind him. Both were apparently surprised, but Robert thought the young man was about to run into him and raised his cane. It accidentally struck the young man's face just before he did indeed run into Robert. That's all Robert remembered, but I think it's enough."

"I thought there were no students here now," Father John said.

"A few are for summer term. I'm guessing this one's a fraternity member and, if so, I'll guess further that it's the frat our young monk was in as a student. It sounds like something they'd think funny: putting a chess piece in the chapel and letting us stew about it — harmless, really, except that Robert was in the wrong place at the wrong time.

"He was a little late for prayer — not unusual for him at his age — but if I'm right, the culprit's planning didn't allow for anything like that. I'll check with our young monk, who, I suspect, purposely left the door open. If that's the case, he'll be chastised just knowing that I figured it out. He doesn't need to know of your help, Father. I think he'll soon be feeling even guiltier than he claims to be now. I'll just have to make sure that guilt doesn't consume him. Thank you, Father, for your help with this." He was smiling as Father John took his leave.

Father John went to his room across the hall and decided to begin his retreat with a short nap, something he rarely did at home but had determined to do on retreat whenever the notion struck him. His alarm roused him in time for Noon Prayer, and he was determined to arrive for it on time. He hoped that would set the tone for all his other prayer moments with the monks.

The silent meal that followed was punctuated only by the sounds of one of the brothers reading aloud from a book by Thomas Merton, a book begun at the evening meal the previous night and one chosen, Father John had learned, largely because a priest was to be on retreat that week.

After the meal, the abbot told Father John that his suspicions had been correct and that all was well now. Nothing more was to happen to the monk; the Dean would verbally chastise the student; and Brother Robert would return soon, apparently none the worse for wear, despite his mild concussion. Most of the monks may not yet know the whole story about Robert's fall — Father John couldn't be sure — but he never learned the identity of the young monk or his erstwhile frat brother.

CHAPTER IV

Father John was finding the monastery routine very helpful for his retreat. During the summers, the monks were at prayer by 6:25 and immediately afterward — around 7 — went to breakfast. Not until emerging from that meal could they break the Grand Silence that began with Evening Prayer the night before.

Daily Mass was at 8, and the monks gathered for prayer again just before noon, going immediately thereafter to lunch. Meals were typically silent, with reading at the noon and evening meals, except for feast days and special occasions. Vespers at 5 was the next prayer moment and afterward, until supper at 6, there was a recreational moment they called Haustus — a Latin word, something not unusual for Catholics in general and Benedictines in particular. Derived from a verb for drawing water or, by extension, for drinking, it was a communal moment at which a variety of beverages, including beer and wine, were available. After supper, they shared another community moment before their 7:30 Night Prayer.

St. Benedict had seen the need for his monks to share time with one another, and after the day's work, just before and after supper, seemed the best time. As far as Father John could determine, St. Martin's monks weren't strictly obligated to be at those two gatherings, just strongly urged to attend. In any event, most of them did seem to spend that time in the common room with their confreres.

After Night Prayer, the house went silent — the Grand Silence — until after the next morning's breakfast. Grand Silence was a time for contemplation and prayer, but it also allowed for preparation of classes for the next day, as well as relaxations like reading, viewing movies or watching television. By chance, Father John had learned from one of the older monks that Night Prayer had recently been reinstated, having had an on-again, off-again existence at St. Martin's. He was rather glad it was in vogue again because he found something comforting about praying for a peaceful sleep and a holy death before settling into the arms of Morpheus.

The entire schedule helped Father John settle into the prayer and reflection of his retreat and, with the Brother Robert incident behind him, he was finally able to begin taking spiritual stock of the past year. Before he arrived, he had asked the abbot to suggest an older priest to serve as director for his private retreat and, upon arrival, was introduced to Father Peter, one of the retired monks. It was in his room that first afternoon that Father John officially began the work of his retreat.

The visiting of rooms — or cells, as they were often called — was ordinarily forbidden, Father Peter explained to him. "But not for something like this, of course, Father."

"Yes, I know. I studied under the Benedictines at St. Meinrad Seminary in Indiana."

"Good. Then you already understand a lot about us. So tell me, then: what specifically do you want to focus on and pray about this week?"

Father John took more than a bit of time recounting the disturbing events precipitated by the skeleton's discovery in Algoma some weeks earlier. "I think I need to get back on an even keel after all that, Father."

"Call me Peter, please."

"If you'll call me John," Father Wintermann said, with a smile.

"Agreed ... John," the older priest said, smiling back at him. "What specifics should we address, then?"

"There are some golden oldies: pride, plus feelings of unfulfillment and underappreciation, though I suppose those aren't as pronounced any more. Now, they're more a kind of treasured monster in the closet, an old adversary comfortably reminding me I'm still myself and not someone or something different. Does that make sense, Peter?"

The monk nodded wordlessly.

"But there's also something new: resentment of authority ... "

Father Peter cut in. "You mean the bishop or something like that? I would think that sort of thing doesn't develop suddenly."

"It's not the bishop or anything like that. It's God."

The monk was silent for several seconds, which gave Father John the opportunity to take a good look at him for the first time. He was hunched with age but alert, a man with very sparkling eyes. In this initial assessment, he seemed bright and caring. In the space of those few seconds, all the old man could think to say was: "That's novel." But he quickly added: "I mean to say that it's not at all what I expected. It's also hard for me to make sense of *that* popping up *suddenly*, either. Help me out: please explain where it came from."

"I don't know if I'm being too deterministic, but it just didn't seem fair to me — and therefore it made no *faith-sense* — for those people to die like that ... especially the one young man, Peter. And as for the trucker's death — I mean, just after he had turned his life around like that — that made even less sense. I don't know exactly when it began. Not immediately after those events, I think, but soon enough I found myself blaming God. And once I realized what I was doing, I got scared. That's not like me, after all. But I couldn't shake it. One thing led to another and, well, here I am. I figured I needed a retreat … and the sooner the better.

"But, in all honesty, even that seems to have taken a back seat to something else. I was — still am — surprised to find that those events have shaken my faith, and more than a little." After a moment, he spoke again. "Or maybe that and the God thing are just two sides of the same coin. I can't be sure."

Both men pondered that assertion.

Father Peter looked at his watch and announced that their discussion was at an end — a little too conveniently, it seemed to Father John when he thought about it later. "The hour's up. We'll come back to this tomorrow afternoon."

Father John was caught off-guard by the abruptness of that declaration and was deciding what to do next: say something, leave or something else. His indecision gave the monk time to add: "Meanwhile, I'm going to suggest something interesting to occupy you before we talk next. I'll ask one of the monks to show you Mount Rainier."

Father John looked surprised and perplexed.

"Don't worry, John," the elderly monk continued, "there's a rhyme and reason for your trip, and we'll talk about it tomorrow. Meantime, go see the mountain up close. It's to be a beautiful day and the mountain should be *out,* as we say here, so you'll be able to see it properly. You'll also find the visitors center there wonderfully informative. Be sure to spend a good amount of time there. Tomorrow, then, we'll talk about the mountain ... and why I think you need to go there."

Father John stood up, perplexity clearly etched on his face. "Tomorrow," he said, resignedly, and stepped into the second-floor corridor.

All the way to his room he tried to puzzle out what the mountain had to do with anything he had told the older priest. He couldn't puzzle it out and gave up trying once he was in his own room again. As was his practice, he had put his watch away for the week, but a glance at the clock in his room confirmed that an hour remained before Vespers, and he decided to walk the outdoor Stations of the Cross that he'd heard about the previous night during what amounted to a general orientation. The leisurely mile-or-so walk around the Stations was exactly the sort of thing to clear his mind while giving him an opportunity and a format for prayer. He felt energized when he rejoined the monks and was no longer preoccupied with the mountain and the morrow.

But at Haustus he was approached by a young monk and brought back to thoughts of his impending day trip. The young man was a seminarian in his next-to-last year of theological studies at Oregon's Mount Angel Seminary, a school and abbey belonging to Benedictines of a Swiss Congregation, not the Cassinese Congregation to which St. Martin's monks belonged. Seminarians there came from several dioceses in the Northwest, as well as from the abbeys of Mount Angel and St. Martin.

"Excuse me, Father Wintermann. I'm Brother Michael. Father Peter asked me to take you to Mount Rainier tomorrow. I gather you've not been there before?"

"That's nice of you, Michael. I recall the abbot mentioning your name last night. You're right. I've never seen the mountain before. Not, at least, 'up close,' as Father Peter put it. It looks awesome enough from here, though, I must say."

"I think you'll enjoy it. I do every time I go there, which is probably why Father Peter tapped me to take you. That, plus the fact that I'm available, being on break from school and all."

Michael was a tall, slender young man with entirely too much hair for the size and shape of his face. Father John found himself wondering as he stood next to him in conversation whether all of it could fit under his cowl, should the young man ever try to keep his head dry in the rain. The young man also had a seemingly genuine smile that he seemed to flash quite readily.

"When *do* you go back, by the way ... to the seminary, that is?"

"Oh, not until right around Labor Day. While I do have a bit of reading in preparation for next term, it's no burden. So I have time to help the former abbot with the flowers around here ... *and* to take you to our mountain, too."

"You like that sort of thing, I suppose? Flowers, I mean."

"Yes. You don't?"

"It's not that at all. I fancy flowers of all sorts, actually, and, in fact, I may have you show me around the grounds to broaden my knowledge of your varieties out here. It's just that, in my experience, few church folks seem to have a similar interest — at least, not in my part of Illinois. One of my fellow priests does, and we often take trips to get our flower fix. It's refreshing, really, to come across someone who does, even if it took me 2,500 miles to find you. Although, I should've figured there'd be at least a few like you in any monastery." He smiled broadly, and Michael followed suit.

"I believe Father Peter wants to see me late tomorrow afternoon. Will we have time enough? If so, when should we leave?"

"Right after morning Mass. That'll give us plenty of time. But you should check with Father Peter as to exactly when he wants to see you, so I don't overshoot the time."

"I'll do that, Michael. But before I forget: how should I dress?"

"Anything casual will do."

"But won't it be cold on the mountain?"

"It'll be cooler than here, but unless you're exceptionally sensitive to temperature changes, a windbreaker should be enough. Do you have one with you?"

"I've a sweater. That okay?"

"Probably, but I'll bring a jacket for you, just in case. Even so, we'll probably be indoors most of the time. Looking forward to it, Father ... and to getting to know you, as well." He smiled again and made his way toward the community room door, joining several others who were already leaving for the monks' dining room in the school's main building across the street.

Seven or eight minutes remained before supper, and as it took only a minute or so to walk to the meal, Father John looked around for the retired abbot, now that he knew of that flower connection. Not finding him in the community room, he moved toward a group of the younger monks, listened politely to their conversation and followed them when they left.

Supper was again silent, and Thomas Merton was, he assumed, properly impressive. Truth to tell, it wasn't his cup of tea. He listened, nonetheless, enjoying the food and trying to appear interested in the book. But what was really occupying him when he wasn't savoring his beef and noodles were thoughts of the mountain's supposed importance. By meal's end he hadn't cracked the riddle of its pertinence and resigned himself once and for all to deciphering that during the actual experience — or, if all else failed, waiting for Father Peter to enlighten him.

CHAPTER V

Next morning, as chauffeur and retreatant met in the parking area behind the abbey, the mountain could be easily seen dominating the eastern horizon. It looked beautiful and beckoning in the sparkling, clear midmorning sky. When Father John said as much to the young monk, Michael acknowledged that perhaps Washingtonians tend to take it a bit for granted. "That's another reason it's good for me to go there every so often, and today's surely a superior day for that. Everything's just right: the temperature, the air and our early start. Knowing that Father Peter wants you back by 4, leaving now gives you plenty of time for the mountain and for Father Peter. Hop in. We get to take the car the abbot usually uses."

"Got all the amenities, does it?"

"Not that many, actually. But it does have power windows."

Realizing that even his aging Taurus had that feature, Father John concluded that the Benedictines in Lacey weren't an extravagant lot, even as to the abbot's car. Keeping that to himself, he engaged Michael in conversation about his seminary studies for the first minutes of the drive.

As they headed toward the town of Yelm on the first leg of their journey to the mountain, Michael spoke easily of what he had been learning, and Father John kept prompting with questions. But twenty minutes later, Michael adroitly shifted the conversation. "What brings you all this way to us out here, Father?"

"I heard about your abbey from one of the younger priests in my diocese. As I recall, he met a priest or two from the Seattle

Archdiocese at some national meeting. I've no idea how St. Martin's came up in conversation but, in any event, he learned about you from them. And when I casually mentioned that I wanted to make a summer retreat, he suggested I look into your place, adding that if I hadn't been to the Northwest yet, I'd fall in love with its beauty. He was right about that, by the way. He also warned me that there'd probably be no set retreat program. But that's not a problem. Many of us go to the Trappists at Gethsemani in Kentucky — you know, where Thomas Merton lived."

Michael nodded. "The book we're reading."

"Of course. Anyway, they haven't provided a set program there for many years now, either, but it's still a wonderfully prayerful place. They do, however, have a very qualified monk or two who offer reflections each evening after Night Prayer. I especially like Father Matthew Kelty."

"Yes, I know. I've been there once," the young man said.

Father John nodded approvingly and continued. "Our diocese provides retreats in either late fall or January. But I wanted to come now because some very unsettling things happened in my town over a month ago, and I was more than a little affected by them. I hope this can get me back on an even keel spiritually again. And though I've talked to Father Peter only once, I believe he can help me with that. Leastways, I hope so."

"He's wise and holy, in my estimation, Father. And he doesn't push himself on anybody. He's not my spiritual director, but others who use him tell me how good he is."

"Glad to hear it. That's reassuring, Michael."

"If you don't mind telling me, what sort of things happened back in Illinois? And while you're at it, can you also tell me about your ministry back there in ... what did you say the name of your town is?"

"Not sure I said it in your hearing, Michael, but it's Algoma. My parish is St. Helena's, and it's in one of two counties in our diocese that are heavily Catholic. Both of them are at the northwestern tip of the diocese near St. Louis. Once you get outside those counties, the other twenty-six are largely Baptist, with a sprinkling of Methodists and Lutherans, plus lots of small Bible churches. I've been pretty much all over the diocese in my assignments, but I've been at St. Helena's for going on thirty years. I've gotten so I can't imagine being anywhere else. I certainly haven't asked to be ... nor have I *been* asked to, either.

"The people in the town are good — and I'm including those in the other two churches as well, the Lutherans and Methodists. I suppose it's already clear how much I love them all." He smiled, sheepishly, but didn't give Michael a chance to comment.

"What happened involved some drug people, and before it was over, several young men and their families were threatened, and one of them died. The whole town was terrorized, really, for over a month before things were brought to justice. Ironically, the man who prompted it all had a genuine change of heart, only to be tragically killed as the police were bringing the mess to a conclusion. I had worked with that criminal — spiritually, of course — and felt very bad about his death, as well as about the young man who died ... and his family, too. It shook me up a lot more than I suspected it could.

And the more that became apparent, the more I decided to do something about it. I must say that just being here and praying with you all has helped some already. But Father Peter and I have a lot more to do."

He fell silent, and his driver decided to let the older man speak when he was ready. Father John finally said: "Tell me more about the mountain."

"It was sacred to the Indians here. They called it Tahoma, which means 'the mountain of God.' I've always liked that."

"You don't say! I like that too. Very much, in fact."

"It's a volcano, you know."

"No, I didn't. Is it active, or just used to be?"

"If you look up and down the Cascade Range, you'll notice several things, Father. The range itself is nowhere near as high as the Rockies, but every so often a large mountain pokes its head up. Mount Baker's north of us, then comes Rainier and, further south, Mount St. Helen's — you remember hearing about the devastating eruption there a few decades ago?"

Father John nodded.

"There's also Mount Hood, and a number of others to the south. Anyway, they're all volcanoes, and geologists assure us that they're all still active. Mount St. Helen's horrible but spectacular eruption is the latest evidence of that. At the visitors center you can soon learn about that sort of thing as well as the last time Rainier itself erupted ... a bit less than two hundred years ago."

He saw the surprised look on the priest's face. "Oh, don't worry. Nothing like that is happening with our mountain currently.

But it could sometime, geologists say. They also tell us that we *should* have plenty of warning beforehand and that any eruption will be a problem to people in the nearby river valleys, especially those formed by runoff from the mountain, but people west of the mountain shouldn't be bothered much, not even by the smoke and ash plume that will certainly form because that will almost surely drift eastward. Although an eruption might trigger or be accompanied by an earthquake, which would, of course, be another matter entirely."

"I didn't know anything about all that."

"I'm guessing that's because there aren't volcanoes in Illinois."

"You're on target there. We certainly don't have any mountains, either, unless you count the Ozarks, which most everyone thinks of as hills, anyway. But I also agree that's why people like me are ignorant of what you all out here must take more or less for granted. You mentioned the possibility of an earthquake. Are there many out here?"

"Oh, yes. In fact, we had a fairly significant one here a few years back. I was a St. Martin's student at the time, and it was plenty scary, let me tell you! It was centered just north of us but came from thirty-five miles or so below the Earth's surface, and the experts said that made it far less devastating than it could have been. A lot of the shock waves were absorbed on the way up, according to them. Nonetheless, it did somewhere in the neighborhood of two billion dollars worth of damage, so it was devastating enough, as far as I'm concerned. I certainly don't want another one! The visitors center at the mountain has lots of information about much of that ... certainly stuff about the mountain, and I think even about that quake."

"You think that's why Father Peter wants me to go today?"

"Frankly, Father, I haven't a clue. But it sounds plausible."

They were well past the town of Yelm by that time, but Michael mentioned it, nonetheless. "Depending on a number of things, we may end up stopping at the town we went through some time ago. I mean, there's a restaurant and inn just before you get to the visitors center up ahead, but I'm not sure it's open — something in the back of my mind says it's under renovation. Anyway, it is a good place to eat. But if it's closed, we may have to make some decisions about lunch. I think there are sandwiches at Paradise — that's what they call the area where the visitors center is — but, if memory serves, they're rather expensive. So if that inn isn't available, we may have to leave early and get something in Yelm to last us 'til supper."

"Actually, Michael, my breakfast was decent. If you can make it that long, I believe I can."

"We'll play it by ear, then, Father." He flashed his trademark smile in reassurance.

"One other thing. When we arrive, we'll be alongside the mountain. The visitors center is quite far below Rainier's peak. Others I've taken here have been surprised to be looking smack into the side of the mountain."

"No problem. But thanks for that information," Father John said.

Both men fell quiet again until they entered the park in which the mountain is located.

"Are we close now?" Father John asked as they pulled away from the ranger station where Michael had flashed a national parks pass that allowed them free entry.

"Close, yes. But there's still a bit of driving. Won't be long, though, 'til you can see Rainier again. We'll be at Paradise then." The mountain had been popping in and out of view throughout their trip, the twisting route alternately concealing and revealing it. It had been hidden for some time now, and Father John found himself increasingly eager to see it up close.

The scenery in the park was spectacular. They were smack in the middle of a large stand of tall evergreens. Father John guessed they were the Douglas firs the monks had mentioned at his orientation. He made a mental note to ask Michael on their way back about the difference between the area's various tall trees: firs, sequoias and redwoods, his memory told him.

Not only were the trees tall enough that he couldn't see their tops from the car, but their trunks were enormous, as well. The tall oaks he was familiar with in the Midwest rarely had trunks comparable in girth and certainly none of them were as tall as the trees he was driving through at the moment. His arm resting on the open window frame of the car registered the increasingly lower temperatures, and he felt a wonderful sense of peace in the forest's quiet, subdued greenery.

They passed the restaurant Michael had mentioned. It was clearly closed ... for *remodeling,* the large sign said. "I guess we're punting," Father John said, acknowledging the sight with a jerk of his head. "Plan B, here we come! But, as I said earlier, Michael, don't let that worry you. I doubt I'll be in any great need of food."

Michael nodded.

As they pulled into the parking lot at Paradise, Father John gasped. Not only was the mountain visible but, as he looked through the car window, it took up his entire field of vision.

Michael noticed his face. "Awesome, eh?"

"I feel a little foolish. I think I should have realized it would be big, but I hadn't really thought about that, I guess. Takes your breath away."

Michael dared a self-satisfying grin, as if to say *I told you so.*

CHAPTER VI

His vision no longer restricted by the car window, Father John stood in the large parking lot and could see how massive the mountain really was. The sight so captivated him that he didn't notice the noticeably cooler air. "Wow! It looks even bigger up close here!"

Brother Michael merely smiled.

"Give me a moment. I want to get the full impact."

Brother Michael was still smiling. "No problem."

Father John moved his eyes slowly from side to side to get the complete perspective of the mountain's massive width, then leaned back against the car and inched his line of sight upward. He found himself craning his neck to look that high. When he finally indicated to Michael that he was ready to go inside, he was rubbing the back of his neck to ease the cramp that had developed there. "It's huge, all right."

Over the next several hours, both men wandered around separately, and Father John lost track of his young driver. He found the exhibits totally fascinating and absorbed everything he could about volcanic activity throughout the Cascades and the ecological importance of that to Washington state. He also found the information about seismic activity throughout the Cascade Range curious and compelling.

It got him thinking about Missouri's New Madrid fault and how its catastrophic upheaval in the early 1800s had affected the states of Illinois and Missouri, even changing the course of the Mississippi River. He had a vague understanding of Renton's location near Seattle and was amazed to discover that Rainier's eruption a decade or two after the Midwest earthquake had sent mud and debris forty miles upriver to form the plain that defines that area. The size of the mountain and the power of its volcano were awesome.

When Michael finally found the priest, he had been sitting for more than thirty minutes thinking about the implications of all those things in the grand design of creation.

"Hungry, Father?" the young monk asked.

"Not really, Michael. I've just been meditating on all this information I feel so lucky to have been exposed to today."

"I wandered around a while but then sat reading for the past couple of hours downstairs. I brought one of the texts I need to cover for next year and I'm almost finished with it," Michael said.

"A fun read?"

"It was okay, in a technical kind of way. Moral theology."

Father John decided not to pursue that, opting instead to ask how much time they had left.

"We could leave any time, though there's another half-hour, if you want to push it to the limit," Michael informed him.

"Actually, I think I'm finished here. We could go now, if you like."

"We can see how your appetite is, then, when we go back through Yelm," the younger man said. But by the time they got there, Father John indicated that they could continue on to the monastery in Lacey.

"I won't waste away before supper," he said. "And if we happen to get in a little early for my appointment, I'll try to see Father Peter ahead of time … while things from today are still fresh."

At the very beginning of their return trip, Michael explained to Father John the difference between Douglas firs, sequoias and redwoods. "We have them all at St. Martin's, plus numerous deciduous trees. But mostly our tall trees are Douglas firs. I'll show you all of them back on campus — that's the best way to tell those three larger kinds apart, I think."

From Yelm all the way back to the abbey, the two fell silent, lost in their own thoughts. When they pulled onto the abbey grounds, the priest thanked his driver. "It was a *very* nice day, Michael. Thanks for making it happen."

"Glad to. Father Peter knows how special the mountain is to me and how much I like taking people there."

As the young man parked the abbot's car in the lot behind the monastery, Father John made his way inside and up to Father Peter's room.

CHAPTER VII

When he announced himself at the monk's door, he found Peter reading a rather smallish book, which his Benedictine spiritual advisor immediately put aside to greet him cheerfully: "How did you like your excursion today?"

"Spectacular! But I'm not telling you anything you surely don't already know."

"Sit down. I want to hear all about your reactions to the mountain."

Father John surprised himself by rattling on for nearly thirty minutes about the mountain's beauty, the impact on him of its size — especially when viewed so up close — and the wealth of geological and ecological information about it and the whole Cascade Range.

When he finally stopped for a breath, he realized that he had been talking for an overly long time, and a sheepish grin spread over his face. "I didn't mean to take up so much time, Father," he said.

The monk merely grinned. "Don't worry about that. It's more or less what I had expected — indeed, had hoped for."

"Is that why you had me to go there? The beauty and size of the mountain?"

"Well, before I answer that, I think you should know that I have another day trip for you. I'll get a different one of the younger monks to take you tomorrow to Priest Point Park just out of downtown Olympia."

"And I'm guessing that you're going to be as cryptic about why you want me to go there as you've been about Mount Rainier." He smiled, expectantly.

"As a matter of fact, you're correct about that. But it'll all become clear soon enough. Meanwhile, I hope you're finding our monastery a prayerful place. I forgot to suggest some Scripture passages yesterday, so please take this sheet and prayerfully peruse them in the order in which they're listed. Don't rush your reflection on any of them, but feel free to move on to a new selection after you've finished reflecting on the previous one. Since you studied at St. Meinrad, I assume you realize this is what we Benedictines call 'lectio' or 'lectio divina.'"

"I do, Father: spiritual reading. Just what I assume you were involved with as I walked in."

"Yes, as a matter of fact."

"Although they told me at Meinrad that it isn't any longer confined to sacred Scripture. Again, like the book you were just reading."

"Correct, again. But, in your case, I want you to read from Scripture — these passages, specifically."

"Certainly. I wasn't questioning you."

"Understood. Feel free, of course, to read other things you may find helpful. Just don't skip these particular readings."

"Want me to finish them all before I see you next?"

"Not necessarily. Read as many as you can and reflect on them before coming back tomorrow afternoon about this same time. Your visit to the park will be confined to the morning, by the way.

You're to be back by Noon Prayer and lunch. I'll so instruct Brother Bruno. He may or may not stay with you in the park, but I'll make sure he has you back by morning's end. That'll give you enough time for my purposes. You may wish to take something to read or a pen and some paper. Take notes if it suits you ... or read ... or just meditate. Also, there are two parts to the park, one on each side of the road. Be sure to see them both."

Father John nodded.

"See you tomorrow, then," Father Peter said, and Father John rose to leave. There was still some time before Evening Prayer, so he decided to step outside for a short walk.

The day was still gorgeous: typical summer weather in western Washington, he had been assured. The temperature was in the low 70s and he felt little or no humidity — so unlike his native southern Illinois. He stepped outside and walked down the hill on the road that led to the property's entrance at College Street. He strolled leisurely, observing the huge trees that comprised the small, forested area to his left and the larger wooded area that stretched some distance to the north off to his right. He had been told about a resident herd of deer that often grazed in the open meadow on his left just east of the small grove of trees, but he hadn't seen it yet, and no deer were in evidence as he walked along that late afternoon. Encountering neither humans nor animals, Father John was freed of distraction as he walked along.

He was delighted with the sight of the towering trees and wondered why he had never felt that way amid any stands of oak or elm in the Midwest. He decided that because he took them so for granted, they didn't affect him the way these trees, so new to his experience, did. *It has to be the novelty! But whatever it is, these huge firs are wondrous!*

As he neared the abbey on his return, the bells were announcing Evening Prayer. The abbey's five bells were more melodious than the three in St. Helena's steeple, and he had begun looking forward to their regular chiming. He went directly into the Abbey church when he reached the top of the hill and, in the few minutes remaining before the start of Vespers, he was able to settle into a prayerful silence. He had always found the slow rhythm of psalms prayed in common to be soothing, whether they were chanted in English or Latin, and he eagerly anticipated the antiphonal prayer a few minutes hence.

Upon arrival at the monastery, he had been invited to sit with the monks during prayer, but he demurred, telling the abbot that he preferred to sit apart, since he wasn't really part of their religious community. So that afternoon, he took his by-now accustomed place two rows directly behind the abbot and waited for the monks to come into the cool and darkening church. In the few moments before they arrived, he reviewed the prayers of the day's Office and realized that one of the Vespers psalms was on Father Peter's list. He resolved to pay close attention when it was chanted.

He had spent numerous retreat moments with the Trappist monks of Gethsemani Abbey outside Bardstown, Kentucky, and had especially liked the fact that they sang the Office there. It was initially disappointing to discover that the chant of the monks of St. Martin's, though they shared the same Benedictine tradition as the Trappists, was spoken rather than sung. They broke into song occasionally — for hymns — except on major feast days, Prior Raymond had told him, when they sang virtually the entire Office of the day. But he had quickly gotten used to St. Martin's particular slow and rhythmic spoken prayer style and found himself that afternoon looking forward to the coming prayer.

He remembered speaking with a monk in Kentucky about the slow pace of Benedictine prayer. The monk was originally from New York and said that, for all his years at the monastery, he still felt impatience with that very deliberate speed. Father John had acknowledged that it wasn't his personal style, either, nor was it that of his fellow diocesan priests when they prayed together on retreats in Belleville. "But when I'm at a monastery like this," he had said, "I find it strangely comforting."

He also found the interior of the Abbey church to be very warm and inviting. Glimpses of outside greenery were available on two sides of the sanctuary and, on a third side, an enclosed Japanese garden projected a calm and serene feeling to worshippers within. The seating was by chairs, not pews and, moveable as they were, Father John wondered, at first, whether their positions ever changed; but Brother Jerome, the sacristan, had assured him that several times a year the monks reconfigured the arrangement of altar and chairs. In a place where tradition was so sacred, he found it interesting that they wanted flexibility within their worship space. The eagle in full flight that adorned the church's podium was another surprise, and one akin to the many pieces of art that lined the walls of the monastery.

Prayer was relatively short that evening, and he was soon with the monks at Haustus. He found himself next to the Sub-Prior, Father Jonathan, at the soda dispenser, and they walked together across the hall into the community room after getting their diet sodas.

"How is it going for you here, Father?"

"So far, wonderfully. I'm working with Father Peter. I notice, by the way, that he doesn't come to Haustus."

"Not often. It takes him a while to walk across to meals, and there often isn't much time between prayer and supper. So he usually ambles directly over to our dining room. I'm surprised, however, not to see him here, what with a bit more time these summer evenings. But he'll be here after supper, I'm sure. He rarely misses that."

"I also can't help noticing that many of you are no longer young. It's like our presbyterate in southern Illinois. We're graying ... rapidly."

"Yes, but of late we've had a few young men join us. Nathanael, Bruno, Justin and Thomas are in temporary vows, and the abbot tells me that we may get one or two other new prospects soon. Initially, as we're checking them out, we expose them to our life here and call them postulants. But I suspect you knew that already."

"I did. I studied in the seminary at St. Meinrad Archabbey during my final six years. When do your postulants become novices, then, Father?"

"That depends, but usually not for *at least* six months."

"Are any of the four you mentioned ready for final vows?"

"Nathanael is already professed. Thomas and Bruno will be in a year. Justin has two years more. He made his first vows some months back."

"You mentioned Bruno. Which one is he? Father Peter wants him to take me to a park tomorrow — Priest Point Park, I believe he said."

"Yes, that's one of our parks here."

"Strange name, it seems to me."

"Not when you find out how it came to be called that. Maybe I'll let Bruno tell you tomorrow. You can have fun trying to figure it out tonight. Bruno's over there, by the way, standing beside Brother Michael and Father William. Have you met any of them?"

"No, not yet. Well, I met Michael, but not Father William or Brother Bruno. Michael took me to Mount Rainier today."

"I'll introduce you. But first let me tell you a bit about William. He's retired now, in part because of health, but he'd been a very successful and beloved history teacher here for many years. Father Justus replaced him when it was decided that he could no longer teach."

"So he's completely retired?"

"As much as any of us monks ever are. There are still a few things he does around the house, like straightening up our snack bar."

"He's in charge of what?"

"The *snack bar*. But, no, he's not 'in charge.' He just tidies it up. Father Richard, our refectorian, keeps it stocked and does all the ordering for it. He's the one officially in charge. But he works through the university food service, so it's not that difficult a job.

Richard just keeps an eye on it regularly and tells the food folks what we need. And, I can tell you, he gets reminded by any number of us if something isn't restocked."

When the Sub-Prior noticed Father John's continued quizzical look, he elaborated. "Just outside our community room, turn left and go to the end of the hall where you'll find our mailboxes plus a place to grab a pick-me-up between meals. That's the snack bar. It has juice, cookies, crackers and cheese, cereal, bread, jam, fruit — things like that. You're welcome to use it, by the way. I'm surprised you weren't alerted to it already."

"Maybe I was, but I don't remember being told."

"Well, anyway, let me introduce you to Bruno and William. You'll find William full of stories, and Bruno's young and eager to please."

Introductions over, Jonathan stepped away with Michael, and Bruno quickly acknowledged that he had already heard from Father Peter about tomorrow's mini-trip. William was adding his praise of the park to the conversation, when Father James, another retiree, joined them. Before anything more than an introduction could take place, however, the supper bell sounded, and everyone started toward the door.

Father John and Brother Bruno paired up, and after they had gotten far enough ahead of James and William outside, the young monk leaned close to Father John as if to impart something confidential. "James is interesting," he said in a near whisper. "He's become quite eccentric at this stage in his life. He was a well-loved pastor in Idaho for more years than anyone can remember but began suffering from Alzheimer's, and the abbot called him back. This past year he's been getting worse and is no longer completely in touch with things ... in the real world, you know. *And* he tends to talk in exaggerated and very formal language. I thought you should know, lest it otherwise become confusing or embarrassing."

"Thanks. But what do you mean by exaggerated and formal?"

"He says 'thee' and 'thou' a lot, things like that! Sounds like an ancient translation of the Bible. It's funny, but we try not to laugh. He's really nice and a very gentle soul." Bruno looked extremely earnest while he had been talking. "And, there's one other thing. Did you hear him singing tonight during Haustus?"

"No, I don't think so."

"We must be having a full moon, because when that happens he usually sings 'I'm Sinbad the sailor man.'" The young man had broken oh so quietly into song, lest James should hear him.

"Shouldn't that be 'Popeye, the sailor man?'" Father John asked.

"Sure! That's why it's so funny." He rolled his eyes and grinned.

"But to make matters worse, he somehow developed a significant allergy. He almost died soon after he returned to us, and it took a while to diagnose the problem. He's allergic to peanuts!"

"I've heard of that — more and more of late, it seems."

"Yes, but apparently his allergy's pretty bad and getting worse. He may have had it a long time, we can't be sure, but now even the slightest exposure to peanuts or peanut products could kill him, we're told. He can't, for instance, even have anything fried in peanut oil. Food service is very careful with our abbey food, as a result.

"Once back here, James became our glazier again, something he had done in his early years here."

"Glazier?"

"He fixed windows all over campus."

"Oh, of course! I knew that, I guess. It just didn't click."

"But that didn't last long. Once we realized how badly the Alzheimer's was affecting him, the abbot didn't trust him with glass-cutting tools or with climbing all over the buildings, poking out of windows — not even on the first floor, let alone on higher stories. So, unlike most of us, he has no house job now. And the rest of us watch out for him. I think he's rather adorable. But not everyone agrees with me."

"I appreciate all that. Thanks, Brother. But as for tomorrow, when should we meet?"

"Right after Mass. I'll drop you off at the park because I have some errands to do for the abbey. But I'll be back around 11:20 or so."

"Downstairs by the cars, then?"

"Right."

They reached the dining room just as the abbot was looking around for Father John, the only guest that evening, so that he could precede the community into supper.

CHAPTER VIII

Father John had always found Benedictine hospitality particularly endearing. In his famous Rule, St. Benedict had instructed his monks to treat each guest as though he were Jesus. The order's hospitality was displayed in many ways besides inviting guests to be the first to dine. Strangers were unfailingly greeted cordially, and whenever people joined the community for prayer, a member always sat beside them to help them manage the books used for prayer. And in medieval times, it was widely known that pilgrims — any travelers, in fact — could always find a bed for the night plus a meal or two at a monastery, no questions asked. The practice is still in vogue, he knew, though few seem aware of it nowadays.

The evening meal was simple but delicious, and Thomas Merton continued to inform and inspire the monks, despite his continued inability to impress the abbey's sole retreatant. Having sat that evening at the abbot's table, Father John walked back with him to the monastery afterward for the continuation of Haustus. He brought up his pending trip to Priest Point Park as they walked along.

"Father Peter's been giving you a real area tour," Abbot Mark said.

"Yes, but he hasn't said why either of these jaunts are important."

"He can be mysterious at times. But trust him to be spot on with his spiritual 'therapy.'"

"I mentioned it to Father Jonathan, and he seemed to take pleasure at not telling me how the park got its name. He said I'd probably find out tomorrow and that meanwhile I might have fun trying to figure it out."

"Sounds like Jonathan. Want me to give you the answer?"

"It might deprive your Sub-Prior of his fun. I think I can wait for Brother Bruno to tell me … while still trying to puzzle it out for myself tonight."

"*If* Bruno knows … " the abbot said, smiling.

"If he doesn't, Father Peter will have to be the one to finally end my torture," Father John said, flashing a small smile of his own.

They reached the community room and Father John took leave of the abbot to make his way over to a lone monk looking at Mount Rainier from one of the sliding patio doors. The mountain was glorious in the evening sun, all pink and majestic: a totally different sight from any other time of day. "Hello. I'm Father John Wintermann, in case you're one of the few around here who doesn't know that already."

"I'm Father Justus. Good to meet you."

"Oh, I just learned your name before supper, though I didn't know which face to match it to. Glad to meet you. Father Jonathan told me that you teach history. But didn't I see you playing the organ at Mass?"

Justus carried himself gracefully and appeared to be very outgoing. "Yes," he said, "that's my second love. I have a master's in the field, but music is my true passion. As a young monk, I was sent to Rome to study music and liturgy. My undergraduate minor in history had to be upgraded when it became clear that Father William was starting to slip. He taught history here before me, if you didn't know."

"So I was told by Father Jonathan. You like teaching?"

"Oh, yes! But the question is, which subject do I enjoy more, history or music? I teach them both."

"And the answer is ... ?"

"The diplomatic answer is both. But, in fact, I enjoy teaching music far more. Going away, it's music, all right. The only problem is, there's not much interest in it among the general student population. I teach only one section, although, I must say, those students are interested and interesting. They want to be there, you know! I have two history classes each term, but few of those students in a given semester are as turned on. Every so often I find appreciative students in my history sections, but generally it's the music students who are the joy of my teaching life."

"How long have you been teaching here?"

"Long enough to be promised a sabbatical in another year. I may have to split it up to accommodate the curriculum, unless they find someone to fill in for a whole year. I want the whole year all at once if I can get it."

"So, where will you go and what'll you do while you're away?"

"Back to Rome for some courses ... in music, certainly, and maybe history."

"And you'll do some touring?"

"Oh, of course ... in Rome itself, but also throughout Italy. I've already begun to set that up, even though I won't leave 'til next

May. What about you, Father? Any travel plans? Other than the Northwest?"

"Not really. I'm pretty much a stay-at-home."

"So what brings you here, then? A lark, or are you perhaps visiting friends or relatives out here, as well?"

"No — just the retreat."

"Seems like a long way to come for that. From Illinois, right?"

"That part of it may have been a lark. I heard about St. Martin's from a priest in my diocese, and since I've never been here before, I decided to try your place, rather than Gethsemani in Kentucky, where I've been numerous times. Your gentle weather sealed it for me. Kentucky's no better than southern Illinois this time of year — too hot and humid."

"We're spoiled, for sure. I guess you know that Rome's a bitch in the summer too — pardon my French!"

"That's interesting."

"Rome's weather?"

"No. 'Pardon my French!' We say that in Illinois too."

"That surprise you?"

"No, but I find things like that curious. I mean, how people talk in various parts of the country."

"Well, then, you must surely be enjoying all the Indian names for our towns and rivers and such."

"Like what? I don't recall hearing any yet."

"Rivers like the Stillaquamish, Lilliwaup and Snoquamish, and towns like Cle Elum, Pe El, Enumclaw, Uptanum, Sedro-Wooley, Breidablick, Mukilteo … and there's Alfalfa and George."

"George? George, Washington? Not Indian, but funny."

"The people there don't particularly think so. But you're right. It *is* funny."

"Most of our oddities have to do with peculiar pronunciations like *El-dow-RAY-dow* and *KAY-row* —- not *El-dow-RAH-dow* or *KAI-row*."

"Oh, we have our share of those. Try pronouncing P-u-y-a-l-l-u-p."

"I give up."

"*Pew-AH-lup*. And there's also S-e-q-u-i-m, which is pronounced as though there's no 'e' in it. Maybe I should do a little something with things like that in my Northwest history class," Father Justus mused. "Are you making the retreat on your own here?"

"No. Father Peter is guiding me."

"He's a good man. Has he sent you to the mountain yet?"

"Yesterday. He does that a lot?"

"I took a wild guess. He loves Mount Rainier."

"I'm going to Priest Point Park tomorrow."

"That's new. Never heard of his especially liking that place."

"Beats me why I'm to go sightseeing. He hasn't clarified that yet."

"Well, not to worry. I'm sure he has a reason. He's very astute about things like that. He's one of our stars."

Father Justus excused himself, and Father John watched the short, wiry man leave the room before going to the large table with all the newspapers on it. He had picked up a copy of The New York Times while awaiting the bell for Night Prayer when he overheard two monks a few feet away discussing in hushed tones someone named Thurman. It was plain that they held little affection for him as they discussed the fact that the man had been 'back' several days earlier, apparently just before he had arrived for his retreat. The conversation ended abruptly when the bell sounded, but Father John found the tone so untypical of the monks, as he had come to know them over the past few days, that he determined to make sense of it in the morning, if at all possible.

After Night Prayer, he remembered what Bruno said about the moon and stepped outside. Sure enough, there was the moon rising above the church, full and beautiful. *How absolutely gorgeous! I wish I had a camera. And how odd that the moon should affect James like that!*

After a few minutes of admiring the sight, he retired to peruse some of Peter's Scripture verses. He finished several before starting to nod and decided to finish more of them the next morning at the park.

CHAPTER IX

The morning dawned crisp and clear, and a slight breeze made the walk to breakfast after Morning Prayer cool and refreshing. Father John lingered outside to look down the hill on which the university's main building was situated. He could see all the way across to the stand of trees surrounding the three residence halls. There in the meadow just in front of the trees were some of the deer he had heard about. Six or seven, including two fawns, were calmly enjoying their own breakfast as they munched the short grass beyond the new library. There were tennis courts between the library and the trees, he had been told, but he couldn't see them from that angle because of the relatively new, red brick structure. He made a mental note to see the inside of that library the next day. After a few more minutes of deer watching, he turned to go into his own morning meal. *What beautiful creatures,* he mumbled to himself.

He ate quickly, grateful that monastery breakfasts were eaten without benefit of readings from Merton or anyone else. When he finished, he had a bit of time before Mass and, accordingly, made his way slowly down into the meadow to see how close he could get to the deer still feasting there. Walking very slowly, he was able to get within thirty feet of the magnificent animals and decided not to press his luck any further. He was able to watch for ten minutes before the bells called him to Mass. *I must tell Father Peter about this. What a lovely opportunity!*

Mass was shorter than usual because former Abbot Innocent did not preach. Afterward, Father John went back to his room for his sweater. He wasn't sure how cool the park would be and realized that he would be alone there several hours. He also grabbed a Bible and Father Peter's list of Scripture readings. Ten minutes later he walked out into the parking area behind the abbey to find Brother Bruno already waiting by a car.

"Hello. Been here very long?" he asked.

"Just got the car unlocked, Father. Ready?"

"Yep."

"Hop in, then."

As they pulled up the incline behind the abbey, Father John said: "I haven't been able to find out why the park is named 'Priest Point.' Do you happen to know?"

"I do. Well over a hundred years ago there was an Oblate priest who came overland all the way from Montreal, I believe … "

"An Oblate? OMI? Oblate of Mary Immaculate?" Father John couldn't believe his ears.

"Yes. Why?"

"They ran St. Henry's minor seminary back in Belleville from the '20s 'til it closed in the '80s or '90s. And they have a large Marian Shrine just outside Belleville. That's my diocese in southern Illinois, in case you didn't know – Belleville — and I studied at that very seminary. What a coincidence!"

"Yes, that's who it was who came here. He spent more than a year living in the woods on that point of land jutting out into Puget Sound. Locals named it because of his stay there. I'm not sure I ever heard his actual name, but he was an Oblate priest, all right."

"What was he doing there?"

"Evangelizing our native tribes, I guess — and anyone else he bumped into, though there weren't that many whites here then. Eventually he went back to Montreal."

"Came overland, you say? Over the Canadian Rockies?"

"That's how I heard it, Father."

"Pretty rugged kind of guy, sounds like."

"I'd say so. Doesn't exactly appeal to me."

"Nor me," Father John acknowledged.

The two were by that time making their way toward downtown Olympia on Pacific Avenue, which soon merged into State Street as it continued on toward the heart of the capital city. Brother Bruno fell silent, allowing his passenger to take in the scenery. The Capitol Building loomed off to their left as they got near the harbor that graces the southernmost tip of Puget Sound. They soon turned onto the street that follows the shoreline northward, and Father John began to admire the small, but certainly expensive, homes that overlooked the water to his left. He had just begun wondering what the view was like from the larger homes high above the road to his right when he caught sight of the sign for the park a block or so ahead. As they turned into the park, he felt immediately dwarfed by the large numbers of very tall trees, some with trunks that would require at least three or four men's linked arms to encompass.

The priest gasped quietly, and Brother Bruno was smiling as he slowed the car to a crawl. "I'll drive slowly through this side of the park so you can take it in, and then I'll drop you in the park's second half on the other side of that road we came in on."

Father John couldn't believe the size of the trees. Some at the abbey and university might well be as large, but the concentrated numbers of them in the park overwhelmed him. He hadn't felt that at St. Martin's and said as much to the young monk.

"If you walk north into our woods at St. Martin's, you can encounter trees this size — and they're similarly dense and abundant, too."

Just before they went to the other side of the park over the bridge above the road, Brother Bruno pointed out an extensive garden of beautiful blooming roses located near a gazebo. "Lots of weddings are celebrated there," he said, simply.

As they crossed the bridge, Father John could clearly see that there was much more of the park ahead, perhaps again as large a plot of forested land as the one they were leaving. There were stands of large trees, and it seemed somewhat less shady. There was also a set of children's swings and slides, as well as several large shelters for picnickers. As on the first side, there were grills and picnic benches, but in the distance he could now see the waters of the Sound peeking through the greenery. Brother Bruno dropped him near the promontory that overlooked the Sound, promising to return around 11:15.

"Want to meet here or somewhere else in the park, Father?"

"Right here, Brother." He waved as the car pulled away and shouted: "Thanks a lot."

He immediately walked up the slight incline toward a protective railing so he could take in the view of the waters below. Houses and a few commercial properties were in plain view on the other side of the waterway, seemingly but a half-mile away. After ten minutes, he retreated to the shade of the trees and, finding it cool but pleasant, decided that he wouldn't need his sweater. He found a wooden glider and was soon gently rocking back and forth on it.

When he next looked at his watch, he was shocked to see that he had been sitting in meditation for over an hour. He pulled out Father Peter's list, opened his Bible and, by the young monk's return, had finished the rest of the assigned Old Testament readings — all of them psalms, including the one from last evening's Vespers. But a number of unread New Testament selections still remained. *This afternoon's work,* he said to himself, over the honking from the abbey's car.

"So what do you think of the park?" Brother Bruno asked as Father John climbed into the vehicle. He seemed eager to hear his thoughts.

"I was overcome by all the beauty. But I found it surprising that there weren't more people. I saw only one older couple using the park for their daily walk. It's such a peaceful place, isn't it?"

"Yes, it is. But I get similar feelings in our woods at the abbey, as well. I should come here sometime and compare the two places."

"Makes me wonder," Father John said, "whether some of our woods in southern Illinois could provide the same experience. Although, I fear they'd often be oppressively hot and full of mosquitoes." He glanced at his watch. "Are we okay on time, Brother?"

"Sure. We'll be back well ahead of the bell for prayer."

They sat silently for a few miles before Father John remembered the cryptic conversation about the man who had 'come back.'

"Brother, last night after supper, I overheard two of your confreres mention someone named 'Thurman.' That name mean anything to you?"

The young man's face took on a guarded look, and he said nothing for several seconds.

"If I've trod where I shouldn't, I apologize," Father John said.

"It's not that, exactly. It's that there's no easy answer. Simply put, the name *does* mean something. But what it means is complicated."

"Maybe I'm being too nosy."

"Well, maybe you should ask the abbot about this. I *can* say that Thurman was a former member of our community. But I shouldn't say anything more, if you don't mind."

"Perfectly fine, Brother. I probably shouldn't have brought it up."

"The Abbot can fill you in … if he chooses to."

Father John's curiosity was definitely aroused, but he was unsure about pursuing the matter. *I'll have to think about that some,* he said to himself.

CHAPTER X

After lunch Father John was still unsure if he should bring up the Thurman matter to the abbot and decided not to, at least for the time being. He went to his room, instead, to read the rest of the Scripture selections — all from the New Testament — spent time praying over them and went to his retreat director late in the afternoon.

"Hello, Father Peter," Father John said, cheerily. "Before anything else, I want to tell you that I finally saw some deer on your property. Before and after breakfast they were in the meadow below the library. I was even able to get within ten yards of them after the meal. Beautiful animals! I can't believe I had a whole ten minutes with them before Mass."

"A bonus, to be sure. We tend to take them for granted here, I'm afraid. And what did you think of Priest Point Park this morning?"

"It's a beautiful and peaceful place. And I learned from Brother Bruno how it got its name. I was tickled by the fact that the priest in question was an Oblate. There are Oblates in Belleville, if you didn't know."

"They have a Shrine to Mary there, don't they?"

"Yes, a big operation. They also ran our prep seminary where I studied. Ran it 'til it closed in the '80s or '90s, as I remember."

"Did you note anything else this morning besides the park's peacefulness?"

"I was in awe of the trees ... their size and beauty, I mean."

"What about the Sound?"

"Beautiful, too, but the trees were what moved me."

"So why do you think I sent you there, and to Mount Rainier?"

"The beauty and massive size of things at both places, I suppose. But if that *is* it, I'm not sure how that addresses my spiritual concerns."

"Well, don't discount the Scripture readings. It's a package deal. But before I begin tying it all together for you, are you reading anything else while you're with us?"

"Yes, and killing two birds with one stone thereby, I suppose. I'm looking over John Shea's book on Matthew's cycle of Sunday readings. Are you familiar with that series of Shea's?"

"Yes, and I like it. Have you listened to his tapes on the stories in each of the gospels? They're a much shorter version of what you're reading but go more deeply into a few of the stories. I find them an excellent companion piece to the books."

"I'm not aware of any tapes. Are they available at religious goods stores? And what are they called?"

"You should be able to get them at places like that — they're put out by ACTA in Chicago, I believe. I definitely recommend them. They're called 'Gospel Food for Hungry Christians' or something like that. To be safe, get just one gospel, not all four. If you like that one, you can always get the others. But I don't want to talk about Shea right now.

"My 'package deal,' I hope, will get to the nub of things for you, and I'd rather pursue that now. You said, in effect, that you have a quarrel with God … "

"I didn't phrase it that way. I said it didn't seem fair for such awful things to happen to my people at St. Helena's."

"Same difference, Father. Perhaps you feel diffident about quarrelling with the Divine, but that's what's going on. Better people than you and I have done that, by the way: saints, to be precise. While it might sound presumptuous to 'argue' with God, it's perfectly fine, really. Scripture gives us more than one story about that sort of thing. For one thing, we can't hurt God's feelings and, for another, God can handle it. You have a quarrel with the Almighty, Father! You think He's not fair."

"Well, I guess you could phrase it that way."

"Not only can I, Father — I insist on it. Let's call a spade a spade! You're having an old-fashioned argument. And it's all right. You know, you can't serve God properly unless you're both on the same page. Y*ou* need to have it out with God and get things clarified.

"I'm guessing you consider yourself a relatively pious believer, one who's never really stepped out of line in terms of any beliefs. Am I right?"

"Fair enough."

"And this situation is something new — and perhaps scary?"

"When you put it that way, yes, I'd say so."

"Well, then, just for the record. Once again, you aren't the first by a long shot for whom this, or something like it, has been an issue. You're in good company! Some of the great mystics have wrestled with God over far more abstruse and difficult matters than yours. So, rest easy.

"But now, tell me in your own words — and briefly — what the issues are in those Scripture readings I gave you."

"Creation — of the world *and* of people — the exodus from Egypt, including the reception of the Commandments, David's kingship — how he acquired it, things, both bad and good, that he did during it — and, finally, psalms, mostly praising God and God's works."

When he paused for breath, Father Peter quickly interjected: "Good. But there was also the 'lex talionis' — 'the law of the talion' — an eye for an eye and a tooth for a tooth, you know."

"Yes, sorry to have forgotten that. Then, in the New Testament: Matthew's three chapters we call the Sermon on the Mount, Matthew's so-called final judgment scene, Luke's parable of the prodigal son and Romans 5 concerning grace."

"Yes, those are the things I wanted you to pray about. Has anything pertinent to your quarrel with God leapt out at you from your prayer?"

"I'm afraid you're going to have to help me here, Father Peter."

"Okay. But stay with me. I hope my exegesis isn't too tightly woven. You'll have to stop me whenever it becomes so.

"The first psalm on your list says that we certainly aren't much in comparison to God, but God nonetheless pays attention to us — in fact, pays a *lot* of attention. Reassuring for you, I hope!

"The other psalms I chose place us alongside all the amazing and stupendous works of creation, like the mountains, the seas and the many wondrous creatures of our world. *Very* reassuring, I hope!

We're right up there with Rainier, the redwoods and Douglas firs — we're as impressive as they are! The psalmist implies as much in admitting and admiring God's custody over us. 'Who is man that You, O God, should pay us heed?'

"But there's no rationale of fairness or justice that brought any of those things, including us, into being. Nothing *demands* our existence in the first place, and certainly nothing demands keeping us in existence ... let alone in any fashion that *you* might deem fitting. Furthermore, if evolution tells us anything, it's that things change and some things even disappear. Totally! Never to be seen again! Gone! Poof! But no qualms or arguments like yours for the psalmist! No, sir!"

He paused to let that sink in.

"Tell you what," he finally said, "I'll let you chew on just that much overnight. We'll get together tomorrow morning at 9:30, then, instead of in the afternoon — to stay on top of this while it's relatively fresh. Okay?"

"Whatever you say, Father."

"But first off tomorrow, I want you to tell me where you are with this so far ... before I continue with the rest of my spiel."

"Okay."

Father Peter read the puzzled look on his retreatant's face and hesitated before dismissing him.

"Is there anything else?"

"Yes, there is. It's a bit of a non sequitur, but I've decided to ask anyway. Last night I overheard two monks talking about someone named Thurman, whom they didn't think highly of. When I asked

Bruno, he said he'd rather I put that to someone like the abbot. Can *you* enlighten me?"

"He left our community recently, and in a chapter meeting right afterward, the abbot told us he had asked him to. But, like Brother Bruno, I don't feel free to speak further about it. Bruno showed good sense there and no small amount of maturity for a young monk. See Father Abbot, if you want more about that.

"Until tomorrow, then! And be ready to give me your reaction to everything so far." He smiled and indicated with a raised eyebrow that their session was ended.

Father John thanked him and headed to his room one floor below.

CHAPTER XI

After supper, as he walked slowly back with the abbot, Father John decided to pursue the matter of the mysterious Mister Thurman.

"I've debated about asking you — and if you think it's none of my business, please say so — but I overheard two monks last night speaking about someone named Thurman. They said he had been 'back.' I was concerned — still am — because they didn't speak in kindly tones, and that seems so untypical of your Benedictine values. I asked Brother Bruno and Father Peter, and both told me very little — other than that he'd been in your community 'til recently — and they both referred me to you."

The abbot walked along in silence for several yards before turning to Father John. "Quite right of them to send you to me. Very sensitive! Thurman — Herbert Thurman outside our monastery, Brother Oswald within it — *was* asked to leave. The Abbey Council agreed that, under the circumstances, he shouldn't stay any longer.

"He'd had several run-ins with one of our older monks, but more to the point, the community didn't like the antagonistic attitude he had developed. He was becoming disruptive to our communal spirit. While it *is* true that Father James' behavior — he's the monk who got under Brother Oswald's skin — has gotten more and more ... shall we say *interesting* ... to be fair, it must also be said that it had become something of a challenge for *everyone,* not just Brother Oswald. But by the time we pulled the plug on Oswald, he was clearly not up to the challenge — if he ever was. And poor James! He's incapable of understanding what provoked Oswald and doesn't know how to respond, either.

"I'm sorry to hear the implication in what you overheard, namely, that he's still a disruptive force, even if, as it would seem, he's not much to blame any longer. I don't wish to know the name of the monks you overheard. But I'll address this with the whole community, I promise, and I'll do it in such fashion that those monks won't know they've triggered my remarks. You're quite right: this sort of thing runs counter to our Benedictine — and Christian — values. Thank you for bringing it to me."

It wasn't at all what he had expected, but upon quick reflection, Father John realized that it was precisely how an abbot should react. *Maybe it* was *none of my business, but at least there'll be a positive outcome,* Father John thought. *I'm glad for that.*

"I hope I've not overstepped my boundaries, Abbot. I'm naturally inquisitive, I'm afraid. You could figure as much after learning the scenario that brought me here for my retreat."

"No offense taken, Father. You've actually done us a favor. This is something in need of addressing."

They had arrived at the community room, and Father John excused himself. Walking across the room, he passed Father Peter, who had just arrived from supper, and thanked him for the afternoon's session, then continued on to the table where Brother Robert was playing solitaire. Though alone at the table, he seemed quite content.

"How are you feeling now, Brother?"

"Fine, thank you … and thanks for rescuing me the other day. That was very kind of you."

"Well, who wouldn't have? I'm just glad I happened to be late for prayer, or goodness knows how long you might have lain there! Mind if I watch you try to beat the odds?"

"Not at all ... unless you'd like to play double solitaire?"

"I could do that," Father John said, sitting down opposite the monk.

Twenty-five minutes went by before Father John glanced at the wall clock and realized that Night Prayer was only minutes away. "I think I'll excuse myself, Brother, and be off to prayer."

"Good idea. I'll put the cards up and follow you. Thanks for playing. The other monks don't take very readily to double solitaire. It was nice to be able to do that for a change."

Father John's slight smile served as silent adieu on his way to the door. He was about to enter the corridor when Father James intercepted him. He was beaming at the chance to talk to someone new.

"Where goest thou, O honored guest?" the old man asked.

Suppressing a smile, Father John replied, "To Night Prayer, Father."

"And knowest thou the direct and, yea, proper route?"

"I do, Father. But thank you for asking."

"Thou hast made a choice opportune, and one that is right, just and availing unto salvation, besides. Go I thence, as well, O esteemed pilgrim." He stressed the last syllable of 'esteemed,' as though he were in some Shakespearean drama, then promptly turned on his heel to walk away in the wrong direction.

Before Father John could speak or even smile, Brother Elwin had caught the old man's arm and deftly pivoted him back toward the chapel. "Let me help, Father. Night Prayer wouldn't be the same without you."

As though nothing untoward had just happened, James grinned, looked up at Elwin and said: "How thoughtful of you, young monk. Wouldst join us also? The gathering will surely rejoice at your company."

With a straight face, Brother Elwin acknowledged his happiness at joining the community to pray for "a restful night and a peaceful death."

Elwin had quoted from the prayer they were about to chant, acknowledging as much with a wink at Father John, who could not help wondering, as he made his way toward the chapel, how that sort of behavior on James' part could be upsetting to anyone. He found it charming and eminently tolerable. *But who knows what issues Herbert/Oswald Thurman had to grapple with during his time here. People are deliciously peculiar — and I do love them for it!*

After prayer, Father John went to his room to ponder the past two days. Against the backdrop of Father Peter's readings and the afternoon session, he sat in the easy chair across the hall from the abbot, mentally lining up all those words and experiences.

His mind, however, soon jumped back to the bloody events of the early summer in Algoma. He had no idea how long he had been thus distracted, but upon realizing it, he made a conscious effort to refocus on the task at hand. The most he could make of everything before drowsiness overtook him was that people are as magnificent as the great works of nature. But that thought, in turn, reinforced his confusion over the seeming lack of justice shown to magnificent people like young Peter and even Gil Wetzel. His anger had begun to slowly simmer again.

He prayed quietly to Mary to help him sleep, undressed and got into bed, but it was another half-hour before he finally dozed off, thirty minutes of frustrating feelings that God hadn't been fair and — worse — could perhaps no longer be trusted.

CHAPTER XII

The next morning as he neared Father Peter's door, Father John encountered the old monk coming down the corridor toward him. "Oh, excuse me, Father. Am I too early?"

"Not at all. Just make yourself comfortable." He opened his door and gestured Father John inside. "I'll be right back," he said and headed toward the lavatory several doors down the corridor.

Father John stepped in and eyeballed the room quickly. On previous visits he had been so focused on the business of his retreat that he hadn't observed much if anything of the surroundings. But with time to spare that day, he felt free to inspect the entirety of the monk's cell.

As he was told in his orientation, it was the same size and configuration as the other monks' cells: one simple room comprising sitting and sleeping areas. It was equipped with a bed, sink, desk and chair. An amazing number of bookcases lined the walls of Father Peter's room, however — many more, Father John guessed, than in the majority of the other cells — and they held an equally amazing number of books. Furthermore, the shelving went from floor to ceiling, and Father John wondered how the elderly man could possibly retrieve books from the topmost areas without assistance.

A quick perusal of titles showed the collection to be eclectic: fiction, spiritual reading, Scripture and even a number of reference works. *What had he taught? Literature, I think the abbot said. I wonder when he retired. I should ask.* He heard Father Peter's footsteps approaching and looked up as he stepped into the room.

"Admiring my stash of books, I see. Do you approve?"

"I'm afraid I wouldn't be a good judge of that. I read an occasional novel, but I'm not one to read that much or all that often, either."

"Nothing to be concerned about either way," the monk said. "But I should apologize for not being ready when you arrived. We all got overnight notes, you see, from the abbot. Ordinarily the announcement of a chapter session involving the entire monastery would simply have been put on our bulletin board, but it seems this one came up suddenly and was considered urgent enough that the Abbot printed up a batch of notes and took them around himself during Grand Silence last night. I found mine, as I suspect most of us did, when walking out my door for Morning Prayer. It had been laid there sometime last night, it would seem.

"*And* I'm going to hazard a guess that you *did* talk to the abbot — most probably last evening. Because, you see, the brief discussion the abbot initiated in chapter concerned Herbert Thurman."

"You're right. I did talk with him … after supper. And he said he was going to deal with the matter on a monastery-wide basis. But he didn't say anything about doing it so quickly."

"Well, that's what he did. The session didn't take long, I must admit, even though there was a short conversation between the abbot and several monks who had questions in search of a few clarifications. But the session was long enough to prevent my being prepared for you. I was also told by Father Abbot to give you the new number code to our doors, and he said, besides, that I could share the gist of what was discussed."

"New combination? Does that change often?"

"Ordinarily not, but it does sometimes when a monk leaves us. I suppose the abbot hadn't deemed that change necessary before now … not, at least, until last night. It's not that he doesn't seem to trust the former Brother Oswald, as you'll hear, but rather it's a kind of reassurance to those few who definitely do not trust him. I wrote it down for you on this paper. Keep it and memorize it as soon as you can. I'm sure that the abbot would then want you to destroy that paper. The new number is to be programmed in by noon today."

"Thank you," Father John said, as he reached out to take the new code from the monk.

"The abbot told us of rumors apparently flying around concerning a recent visit of the former Brother Oswald to our monastery. The rumors, he said, made that visit sound ominous and unsanctioned, but it wasn't that at all, according to him. As a matter of fact, he went on to tell us, Herbert came back to talk to him — the abbot, that is. He even shared the essence of that discussion, namely that Thurman, having had time to think over his dismissal, felt the need to apologize to Father James as well as to the community for his previous behavior. He wasn't asking to be readmitted, but he wanted the abbot to know that he felt ashamed of his behavior and wanted him to share that with the entire monastery. *And* he said he wanted to be able to say that to Father James.

"But, the abbot told Thurman that it would be best that he and James not get together, that James' condition wouldn't allow him to process what Thurman might want to say, and it might even upset James further. The abbot then promised to convey Thurman's apology to James. According to Abbot Mark, Thurman understood and accepted that.

"Finally, the abbot promised him that he'd tell all the monks about their conversation. Then he apologized to us for not having done so sooner. It seems that Thurman and he had talked four or five days earlier, and the abbot was simply waiting for an opportune time when there would be more than just that matter to share with us in chapter.

"Knowing about your concerns in this regard, Father, I'm guessing that your conversation with the abbot convinced him to talk to us right away, rather than wait for a few more topics.

"In essence, he wanted us to know the whole story so we'd not only understand Oswald's change of heart but stop rumor-mongering. That sort of thing isn't conducive to brotherly love, I'm sure you can see."

"Thanks, Father. I'm glad I had an unwitting hand in that."

"Yes, apparently you did. But, unless you have any further comments or questions on that, I'd like to get on with what you and I are supposed to be about."

"No, I don't. I'm fine. Thanks for letting me know all that."

"Good. Then, are you prepared to bring me up to speed on your reactions to everything we've discussed?"

"I am, I think."

"Please fire away."

"Well, the clearest thing is that people are as magnificent as all the works of nature. And then, as you said, Scripture doesn't indicate that any of that is owed to us. In other words, there's no question of 'fairness' or 'justice' in the equation of creation. But, I'm sorry to say, I still can't escape *feeling* that it somehow plays a role here."

"Correct about the points I've made with you so far. And honest enough on your part that you're still mired in those feelings of unfairness. So, to continue: I'm sure you know the lex talionis, the law of the talion?"

"An eye for any eye … ?"

"Yes. Have you ever reflected on its connection to the Sermon on the Mount? I mean, that part where Jesus not only tells his followers to go the extra mile, but also the one where He says they should love others, even their enemies? He even went so far as to make it — love — the basis of judgment in that famous story in Matthew 28."

"I've never made that connection."

"Moses gave the Israelites that law or rule to get them out of the endless revenge Semites were mired in. Not sure it worked, since they are still mired in it, if the situation in the Middle East right now is any indication. Nonetheless, that's why he did it.

"Jesus came along and asked his followers, in effect, to grow up religiously. He asked them to get over grievances, to forgive, even to forgive enemies. And, for the record, I'm not sure that has worked very well among us Christians, either. But, at the very least, you can see the progression of moral teaching in Scripture, can you not?"

"Now that you point all that out, yes, I can, Father."

"Well, there's more — as I guess you suspected. There's Romans 5. You've probably not connected all those things with Paul's insights on grace in Romans 5, I'm guessing."

"Can't say I have. Got me again!"

"Let me allow Paul Riceour, then, to show that connection. In a wonderful article in Christian Century a number of years back, he identified the logic of Moses' law of the talion as the logic of *equivalence*, and the logic of Jesus' Sermon on the Mount as that of *superabundance*. And he used Romans 5 to make that clear.

"Riceour, by the way, is a Protestant thinker, if you didn't know, and a very good one. It's the 'how much more' in Romans 5 that serves as the linchpin for him in this matter. God goes the extra mile, as it were, all the time, loving us prior to any virtuous behavior *or* sinful actions, and doing so with love that knows no measure."

"That much I'm aware of, Father: that God loves us immeasurably. But that's a part of the problem … "

"Hold on, Father John. A bit more from me, please. I said that Jesus asked his followers to 'grow up religiously.' The logic of equivalence is essentially a child's approach to things. God's logic of superabundance is akin to that of a grownup. Think about it: grownups, under ordinary circumstances, overlook a lot of things, especially in raising children, don't they? Because they know that children aren't capable of understanding a number of things, can't emotionally rise above some things yet and are essentially in a defensive mode while they're growing up. So they tolerate a lot of things, parents do — while patiently nurturing their children and calling them to increasingly mature stances.

"In essence, that's what Jesus asks of his followers, asks of you and me: to let lots of things go, to overlook and even, when it comes to that, to forgive thoughtless, immature, selfish and defensive people. I know it's not easy, but that's the ideal Jesus holds out to us all."

"So I should just overlook those unfair things ... "

"I'm going too fast, aren't I? My argument's too tightly woven, isn't it? I'll slow down, and we'll go back over a few things.

"Let's try this. Have you ever thought about forgiveness as something done from a position of strength?"

"No, I haven't."

"Well, think about it. God can't really be hurt by our sins, right? With that in mind, it's easy for Him to forgive us, since we've not really hurt or damaged Him. In fact, the only ones we hurt by our sins are ourselves, right? In much the same way, parents aren't hurt by the foibles of their children either, are they? From their position of experience and maturity, they know that childish mistakes can only hurt the children, if anyone. So they can overlook those boo-boos and forgive their kids ... with the hope that they'll eventually turn into responsible adults who, having learned from the understanding and loving treatment their parents gave them what works and what doesn't, will have their own internal reasons for avoiding childish mistakes and for making the right choices in their lives.

"So far, so good?"

"Yes ... but where's this leading?"

"Like parents, who only want the best for their children, God only wants the best for us. But also like parents who understand that they can't force their children to behave correctly, God not only knows that we can't be forced, but gave us our free will in the first place. God wants the best for us and wants us to grow to understand what that 'best' is ... and to have the willingness, therefore, to do it ... *on our own.*"

"And fairness ... ?"

"Fairness isn't even in that equation, is it? Parents aren't being either fair or unfair when they eventually let go of their kids' hands, so to speak, and let them walk on their own. They're letting them find out for themselves — after feeling satisfied that they've given all the proper guidance they can. And then they — perhaps reluctantly in some cases — wait with baited — and, certainly, loving — breath to see what happens. Most of the time, by the way, things turn out fine. But in those instances when they don't, the parents can take refuge in the realization they did the best they could ... *and the rest is the responsibility of their children.*"

Both men fell silent, Father Peter waiting — hoping — for some sign from his retreatant that things were beginning to make sense.

The next words came slowly from Father John. "Are you saying that free will is the key to this?"

"One of the keys, certainly."

"So ... Gil Wetzel ... ?"

"The way you spoke of Mister Wetzel, he came across as someone who had made bad choices — a lot of them — but who then came, in time, to realize his mistakes and changed for the better ... in a very big and touching and real way, as you told it."

"But young Peter was dead ... "

"And you want to blame God for that? That *was* your mindset when you arrived here, wasn't it?"

"Yes ... "

"Do you still think it *fair* to blame God? It seems to me that God let Wetzel discover on his own how bad, how *unworkable*, those things were. And Wetzel learned ... and changed ... which was good, wasn't it?"

"Yes. But, as I said, that young man died!"

Father Peter sat silently for some moments, and Father John kept looking expectantly at him.

"We've been going on a long time. And you've begun to put the pieces together, I think. I hope you won't think it cruel to suggest stopping for today at this point. I want you to continue thinking things over, including the one remaining piece, namely, the young man's death. Let's see each other tomorrow at 9:30. I'm hoping that can be our final session. But, if it isn't, we'll continue talking as long as needed. Okay?"

With a look on his face that indicated less than full enthusiasm, Father John agreed. But before leaving, he knelt before the older monk and asked for his blessing.

Slightly surprised, Father Peter gave it and, gently smiling, helped his retreatant to rise. "Go in peace, Father. See you tomorrow morning."

Father John went directly to chapel to continue his praying and pondering, and he was still there more than an hour later when the monks filed in for Noon Prayer.

CHAPTER XIII

Father John's afternoon promised to be long and full of more pondering. But one thing he knew for sure. He had to call Betty, the church secretary at St. Helena's. And he'd better do it as soon as possible ... the first thing after lunch. He realized that he was going to be staying at St. Martin's longer than scheduled, and she needed to know.

Too ambitious a plan, he thought to himself. *Should have known better than to try to pull this off in less than a week!* Never before had he gone on retreat with so much spiritual equanimity at stake. Jaunts to Gethsemani could be made between weekends: three to five days for some spiritual R/R. This was different, as he should have realized. From one Monday to the next simply wasn't time enough for an agenda like this. If that wasn't obvious before, it was surely crystal clear now.

But before I call Betty, I'd better check with my travel agent. Father John wasn't certain that he could get his ticket changed ... not without a serious price hike, that is. *No problem,* he was told. *It's only a* slight *fee to rearrange your ticket, Father. Not to worry!*

Relieved, he dialed Algoma with the calling card he had received the previous Christmas. He'd have to get Betty at home because she didn't come to St. Helena's on Fridays. It was much too late to readjust the weekend's bulletin, he knew, but he could have her tell Tommy to announce the cancellation of next week's daily Masses and explain that Father John was delayed in the Northwest. He could give a full explanation once he returned.

Tom Marano was one of the priests at the retirement facility outside Belleville, and while Father John was grateful that he and most of the others there were available to help on weekends, he knew that they would make sure he'd never hear the end of having extended his trip. *I'll deal with that when the time comes! That conversation at the Home should be good for at least two drinks sometime soon.*

He had changed his flight from the coming Monday to the Friday later in the week. That should be — had better be — enough time. *I've got to get a handle on this thing or I'll be in a* real *pickle!* He would have ample time to prepare for the weekend of his return because, when he flew out of St. Louis on the four-hour-and-some flight, he had spent much of his time in the air doing the first draft of that next weekend's homily. *If I'm lucky, maybe I can finish here at St. Martin's and even have time to see a bit of Seattle ... if I can get there. Possibly one of the monks can take me.*

The real problem — and I know the retired guys will probably say it to my face — is that I hate being away from St. Helena's. His love affair with his cat-lickers at St. Helena's, most of the priests in the diocese knew, went well beyond the ordinary kind of attachment that the bulk of the other priests had to their flocks. *They'll survive without me, I suppose. For goodness sake, they* surely *will! Who'm I kidding? It's just that I miss them, darn it! But I'll survive too, won't I! What was I thinking? I should have given myself more time in the first place ... to see the area here, if for no other reason. If I had, I wouldn't need to be calling now — I'd have the extra time ...*

Betty answered and expressed surprise at hearing his voice. "Where are you? Back already?"

He quickly explained that he was still in the Northwest and would be extending his stay.

"I'll make sure this weekend's announcements include those cancelled daily Masses for next week, then. Anything else?"

"Not really, except to find out how things are going."

"Same old same old! Summer's nice and slow ... even if it continues to be hot and humid."

"No change in that department since I left, I guess."

"Right. And no changes in sight, either ... not according to the TV weather people, at any rate."

"Well, I'm not surprised. See if you can bring in some cooler air by the time I return a week from today, though. I'm getting used to the nice weather out here."

"Should I tell Don the new date to pick you up, then?"

"Oh my gosh, yes. I totally forgot about that. Tell him I won't be coming in Monday, but will arrive, instead, at the *same time* on *Friday*. I think it's the same flight number as Monday's, but that doesn't really matter, I guess. It's the arrival time that's important, and I'm sure it's the same as on Monday. Just tell him to meet me at the same place about twenty-five minutes after the scheduled touch-down, just like before."

"Got it. Enjoy the extra time."

"If 'enjoy' is the right word, Betty! See you soon enough. Thanks for taking care of all this stuff."

When he hung up, his state of mind reverted almost immediately to the muddled confusion he had been experiencing in increasing measure since he began talking with Father Peter. He decided that a walk outside couldn't hinder his sorting out the stuff of those discussions and, with luck, might even help.

He headed down the hill toward the school's entrance on College Street, intending to turn left just before College Street to make the circuit past the residence halls and eventually return either up the Grand Stairway that was the formal entrance to the school or back up the hill past the library to the main building. Once outside, however, something pulled him toward the outdoor Stations instead, and he proceeded to slowly make his way around that circuit. Initially he paid little if any attention to the Stations themselves and kept his mind on the business at hand. But after thirty minutes or so of slowly walking past the scenes of Jesus' Passion and puzzling over the things Father Peter had been saying, he stopped for breath at the eleventh Station and looked up.

The scene depicted Jesus lying on the cross with a soldier kneeling beside him about to hammer a nail into his hand. A quiet voice inside him said *that's not fair!*

He was stunned and stood staring several minutes at the scene, in something like a stupor.

CHAPTER XIV

"Well, well, well!" said Father Peter, who had agreed to see him on the spur of the moment. "We don't have much time, I suppose you know. Evening Prayer is in fifteen minutes."

"I know. Thank you for seeing me on such short notice."

"So it was the Stations that jarred something loose, eh?"

"Yes. It should have been pretty obvious, I suppose, and I should have realized it all along, I'm ashamed to admit: Jesus' death wasn't fair either ... or his Passion. And I don't know of anyone — certainly not myself — who would even dare trying to blame God for it. I can see how you've been right about fairness being nowhere in that equation. I mean: fairness is the wrong issue to raise, the wrong question to ask, isn't it?"

"Of course."

"But ... but I'm still not sure that ends it for me. Where do those feelings come from? And why are they lingering with me?"

"There's still good reason to meet tomorrow, isn't there? Aside from the fact that we don't have any time right now, there's the possibility that continued prayer might jar more things loose. See you tomorrow morning, then. Okay?"

"Right. But thanks again for seeing me just now."

"Glad to. Let's be off to prayer."

The two walked silently together down the corridor toward the elevator and from there into the chapel a few minutes later.

Supper was a nervous affair for Father John. He couldn't concentrate on putting all the pieces neatly together. Thomas Merton kept getting in the way, crashing through every time he thought he was anywhere near to tying everything up neatly.

He avoided Haustus after supper and went directly to his room. And, while he emerged to go to Night Prayer, he returned immediately afterward and spent another hour or two trying to figure out the roots of those persistent feelings. He was yet to claim success when he finally turned out his lights and went to bed.

CHAPTER XV

After Morning Prayer the next day, Father Peter came up to him at breakfast and whispered: "I didn't sleep well last night, and I want to take a nap this morning. Would you mind putting off our get-together until this afternoon? And, just to be safe, can we set it for 3:45 ... in case I need a second nap? Is that okay?"

"Whatever you say, Father. I've more praying and perusing to do, anyway."

"Good. See you this afternoon."

When Father John emerged from the meal, he decided to see the inside of the library and spent over twenty minutes looking around at its rooms, computers and impressive number of shelves. He particularly liked the upstairs periodical room and the miniature bronze sculpture of monks there. *I should find out where they got that.* But he was surprised at what seemed to be a rather sparse number of books on the shelves.

On his way out, he stopped at the circulation desk to inquire about the dearth of books and was told that the pledge drive a few years earlier had contained no provision for acquisitions. "They just asked for enough money for the building, so we're still working on that phase of our library expansion, Father," the clerk at the counter informed him. "We've made a bit of progress, actually, in the past year or two."

"It must have looked quite bare when you opened, then, I'm guessing."

"It did, yes. This building has gobs more space than our former area in the main building. If you have any books to donate, keep us in mind."

Promising to do so, he stepped outside and made his way back up the hill into the main building. Realizing he hadn't really been inside it, either, he spent the next half-hour wandering its halls. The dining facility on the lowest floor seemed impressive and inviting, and he especially liked the new addition to its dining area. The upper floors held numerous offices, but mostly he walked past a lot of classrooms. On the second level he found the campus ministry office. It was open, but he didn't see anyone around. *No doubt the lack of students for summer term,* he mused.

He went next into the cool confines of the Abbey church, instead of to his room, determined to pray there until his time with Father Peter. But around three, wanting something cool to drink, he made his way back into the monastery and down to the first floor in the direction of the snack bar.

When he got to the lowest floor, the other end of the corridor was full of black robes. Five monks or more were spilling out of the large room into the corridor, but there didn't seem to be much sound coming from them. When he got to the group, he discovered that they were indeed silent, and they were all peering into the snack bar.

He asked the nearest monk what was going on. It was Brother Nathanael, one of the postulants, who turned to say quietly: "It's Father James. He's on the floor in there, and I don't think Elwin can revive him." The young man had a troubled look as he turned back toward the center of attention, and Father John could then see for himself that Brother Elwin was stooped over a black-robed figure lying on the floor several feet inside the room.

Moments later, everyone made way for Abbot Mark, who knelt down beside the old man to anoint him. When he stood up, he told the group quietly: "He's gone."

He looked at the Prior. "Raymond, please see to the tolling of our bells."

The monks closest to James silently picked up the old man's body and carried him to the nearby elevator. As the abbot stepped into the corridor after them, Father John spoke quietly to ask if he knew what happened.

"Apparently he had a heart attack and fell onto his face. His nose is bloodied and his lip is swollen. My guess is that he went instantly."

"Was it usual for him to use the snack bar?" Father John asked.

"Not that unusual. He loved jelly sandwiches, and there was one on the floor near him. Poor fellow. I'll miss him. He was such a delightful eccentric of late. But way back when, he taught languages very successfully here in our high school. And then, when we closed the high school in the '70s, he began a second career of sorts as a pastor in Idaho, his home state. The people there absolutely loved him. I must remember to get word to those parishioners right away. Once, that is, we contact his family and make the funeral arrangements. To give them enough time to arrange to come, I don't imagine we'll be able to bury him before Monday or probably Tuesday."

"I hope you aren't offended, Father Abbot, but would it be possible for me to briefly see his body?"

"That's an odd request, Father. I must ask why you want to do that."

"Well, as you know, I've been involved in several strange deaths over the past year, and something I observed as Father James' body went past reminded me that about a year ago I'd noticed something about Annie Verden's body ... something others had failed to note."

"And that would be ... ?"

"Well, in her case, her skin was pinkish in color. Most people would think that indicative of a mild exposure to the sun. But I happened to know that she avoided the sun and, in fact, had not been out in it at that time. But even I didn't put things together immediately, though I did eventually. She died of carbon monoxide poisoning, and that causes a pinkish tinge to the skin."

"And Father James looked pink to you?" the abbot asked, incredulously.

"Oh, heavens no! But, as with Annie, I think there's something that has gone unnoticed. You said his lip was swollen."

"I did ... "

"Actually *both* lips were swollen, Father Abbot."

"Perhaps. So what?"

"I don't think that was caused from falling and hitting the floor."

The abbot remained silent, listening.

"And, though I'm certainly not a medical person, I don't believe that sort of swelling would happen to the degree it seems to have just now. Not from a fall, and not that suddenly, either — in fact, perhaps not at all. But that should be easily determinable, especially if an autopsy is judged in order. Brother Elwin will be upstairs with the body, won't he? We can bring him in on this."

Father John stood expectantly gazing at the abbot, who looked increasingly concerned and disconcerted.

"It surely can't hurt to take a quick look at Father James' face, can it?" Father John said.

"As you say, it can't hurt. Come with me."

They took the elevator and were soon in Father James' third-floor room. His body had been carefully laid on his bed, and Brother Elwin was straightening the old man's habit. He looked up, surprised to see the abbot.

"What is it?" he asked.

"Would you mind staying here with Father John and me a few moments?"

Elwin nodded.

The Abbot then turned to the several monks who had carried James and asked them to step outside. As the last of them quietly closed the door, the abbot explained to Elwin why he and Father John were there.

By that time, Father John was able to point out to the two monks that both of Father James' lips were swollen, and rather noticeably, at that. "Brother Elwin, is it your opinion that swelling like that would likely be caused by a fall?"

"Well, now that you mention it, it's not that probable, Father."

"Well, I don't wish to sound alarmist, but it seems to me that we can't rule out poison, can we?"

The look on the abbot's face spoke volumes. "That's all we need: a monk of our abbey poisoned! Think of the headlines!" After a moment of shocked silence, he added: "And think of the disruption that would almost certainly cause to our monastery routine!"

"Abbot, I merely suggest that we can't rule it out. You could authorize an autopsy in hopes that it's not that. But if it is, the police can be called in good time. In fact, they'll come almost unbidden, is my guess, if poison is indicated. But first things first: an autopsy can be done relatively quietly, can't it?" Father John looked from one monk's face to the other.

Brother Elwin spoke up. "I think I can get that to happen."

"Of course, it could even be that peanut thing, couldn't it?" Father John was desperately trying every form of damage control he could think of, now that he saw how agitated the abbot had become.

"Yes, but he had been eating a jelly sandwich," Elwin said. "No sign of peanuts, peanut butter or peanut anything. Although, perhaps we should seal off the snack bar and do a thorough search to be sure that's what he had ... just in case."

"You might also want to quiz every member of the abbey as to whether they used that facility, and if so, when ... as well as what they ate or did there at the time," Father John said. "All that might — I say *might* — be useful information should this get complicated. It certainly won't hurt to get that information in hand and have it ready."

"Good idea. Elwin, please take care of that now," the abbot said. "And put the snack bar off-limits until you're through. You can alert the Prior and have him take over the details so you can get back up here with James. Then you'd better work on that autopsy."

"Will do."

It amazed Father John how quickly the machinery had been set in motion.

CHAPTER XVI

"Of course," the abbot said softly, as he and Father John were walking back to his quarters, "if it *is* a question of poison, I just know the monks are going to suspect Herb Thurman. I hope we don't have to start all that up again."

"I am sorrier and sorrier I even mentioned the word, Abbot. But it just popped into my mind. And while there is an outside possibility of that, it's highly unlikely in a monastery — at least not a deliberate use of it! All I really wanted to do was suggest that what we saw with the naked eye might indicate something more complicated than a simple heart attack. I could easily be wrong, of course, but I still think it's better to check out all the possibilities than to just assume that it was his heart — especially given things hard to explain, like those swollen lips." Father John was beside himself over the can of worms he had opened.

"If it's any consolation, you've convinced me to check into it," the abbot said. "But ... if it wasn't his heart *or* poison, then what?"

"Peanuts?"

"Not likely. I know that there are no nuts of any kind in the snack bar, and the peanut butter is deliberately hidden high up on one of the topmost shelves so that he couldn't get to it. Those who want it know where to look. For the sake of simplicity, I *do* hope it was his heart."

Father John nodded in silent agreement. "If you don't mind, I'll be off. You have phone calls to make, and I think I've caused enough consternation already." It was with a sheepish grin that he made his departure from the abbot's doorway. But as he turned to go, he looked at his watch and exclaimed: "Good grief! I'm late for Father Peter."

The abbot called after him: "I doubt that Peter knows about James yet. Be sure to tell him. But do so gently. They were close."

Father John waved over his shoulder in assent as he opened the stairway door to head up to Father Peter's room.

When he arrived at his retreat director's room, he knocked and said: "It's Father John. Sorry I'm late."

"Come in," sounded from within.

"Let me tell you something, Father," he said as he stepped inside, "because you may not have heard yet. It's about Father James."

"What? Did something happen to him?"

"Yes, I'm sorry to say. The abbot wanted me to tell you that he dropped dead in the snack bar. As we speak, Abbot Mark is trying to find out if it was his heart or something else."

"How sad! I liked James. We were junior monks together. I will miss him. Let's say a prayer for him, please." Father Peter led them both in the Our Father. He was silent for several seconds before asking, "Will it inconvenience you if we don't have a session at this time?"

When Father John didn't respond immediately, Father Peter added: "How long are you staying with us here? Will putting this off get in the way of your travel plans? Because, if it will ... "

"No, not at all. I'll be around for nearly another week."

"Good. Then, if you don't mind, I'd rather be alone right now," the monk said.

"I understand. When should we get back together, then?"

"Let's tentatively say tomorrow afternoon. Sunday is a slower day for me and for most of us here. What about 4 o'clock or a little before? We can then go right to Vespers."

"Fine. Sorry to be the one with the bad news. See you here tomorrow around 4." Father John nodded slightly as he stepped into the corridor and gently closed the door.

As a boy, Father John had espoused the stereotypic romanticized view of monasteries as being dark, Gothic places with many rooms, some of which were secret or hard to get to, plus some subterranean tunnels. Having studied at the Indiana seminary of St. Meinrad's Archabbey, he realized that wasn't even close to the truth. He had further destroyed that romantic notion at Gethsemani in Kentucky while on retreat there. He got to see a good deal of that monastery while working with the monks in their cheese and fruitcake venture and knew that, like St. Meinrad's, Gethsemani was a utilitarian set of buildings with no surprises built into the architecture.

But he found himself now wishing that something like that might be true about St. Martin's, convinced more and more as he was that Father James' death was not as straightforward as a heart attack or some such natural cause. If his hunch came anywhere near to being right, a secret passageway or a hidden room or two might be the precise thing to help crack whatever riddles might then ultimately turn up.

But as he walked back to his room, he knew that couldn't be the case. He had been all through St. Martin's compact monastery, far smaller than either the sprawling Indiana monastery or nearly-as-large Kentucky monastery. There was nothing even remotely suggestive of secret places from which to pop out of at just the right moment. He also felt that, even though he had been there less than a week, he knew the monks who resided there well enough to say that they were above suspicion, as well. Nonetheless, something sinister did seem to be afoot. And he was nowhere near putting his finger on it.

After that evening's supper, Brother Elwin told the abbot that there were hives or hive-like protrusions on one of James' legs and on his back, and the abbot shared that with Father John after Night Prayer, hoping that he might be able to make sense of it.

"Elwin isn't sure what to make of that, but he's fairly certain that hives weren't a problem that Father James suffered from. Do you make anything of it, Father?"

"Sorry, but I don't. Though it does confirm to me that an autopsy's the right way to go. Do you know when one can be performed?"

"Absent any urging from us — and I'm not giving any — the county won't do it until Monday. I suppose we'll know by that evening. They didn't say exactly what time they'd perform the procedure, by the way, just that it would be Monday."

"Is it too soon to know what turned up from questioning the monks about the snack bar?"

"It is, though Raymond should have that for me by tomorrow. Some monks rarely use the place, although everyone does go into the first part of the room for mail and messages. What about yourself, Father. Have you been in there?"

"Only to peek in, once I learned of its existence. That was a couple of days ago. I was actually on my way there at the time James was found."

"I'll tell Raymond to add that to his report."

"You mentioned a jelly sandwich. Was that correct?"

"Yes."

"Nothing else on the sandwich?"

"Nothing. Which is consistent with James' habits. He loved jelly sandwiches and even with his advancing Alzheimer's knew not to mess with things like nuts or peanut butter. Anyway, as I think I said, there are simply no nuts of any kind in that room, and the peanut butter's up too high for him to reach. He was deliberately kept unaware of the place we keep it, anyway."

"Maybe I'm being too melodramatic, but did you think to keep that sandwich, in case the police might need to examine it?"

"I don't know. I'll have to ask Elwin or Raymond."

"Might want to do that soon. It may need retrieving if it *was* thrown away already."

"I'll do that right away. Thanks. See you tomorrow — at Morning Prayer, I assume?"

"Yes, I'll be there."

"Don't forget: it's a little later on Sundays."

"Oh, yes. Thanks. That wasn't on my radar. The schedule's in my room, isn't it?"

"Should be. If not, you can find it on our bulletin board. See you in the morning, then. Pray for James, please."

"I will. And I have already ... with Father Peter. But thanks for the reminder. I'll be sure to do that. Goodnight."

Unable to sleep, Father John's mind was racing. *I hope it wasn't poison. I don't want to deal with another murder. And it might not go well for the abbot, either, come to think of it. He seems to like Herbert Thurman, despite the fact that he wasn't material for the monastery here. Maybe* like *is too strong a word, but whatever the right one is, he seems convinced Thurman didn't do something like that ... perhaps even* couldn't. *At any rate, I hope this turns out a lot more beneficently than it now seems it might. Let's hope it was an unfortunate accident or something entirely natural, like the heart attack the abbot originally thought had taken place.*

It was another twenty minutes before he finally fell asleep, something he would be grateful for in the morning, given the extra sleep he was allotted before Sunday's Morning Prayer.

CHAPTER XVII

On the possibility that Father Raymond's task might be finished by then, Father John went to the abbot's quarters twenty-five minutes before Sunday morning's Mass. The abbot told him that all the inhabitants of the monastery had been quizzed and that nothing untoward had turned up. Of the eight monks who had used the snack bar within the forty-eight hours before Father James' death, only two of them had eaten any peanut butter, and both had cleaned up after themselves. And nothing was left on the counter that might suggest or lead to foul play.

"If it was poison, Father, either someone's not 'fessin' up to Raymond or we had an intruder. And if the latter, he either got very lucky in passing on his poison to James, or it didn't matter to him whom he killed. But, you know, I just can't bring myself to believe anything along either of those lines."

"Once again, Abbot, I'm so sorry I even suggested it."

"But you've put the bug in my head, and now I've got to track down all the possibilities to satisfactorily rule it out. So I've called Herb Thurman. He and I will meet tomorrow to talk about this. I've not told him why I want to see him, and we'll meet in town so that I don't needlessly stir things up about him with any of the monks."

"That sounds both wise and prudent, Abbot."

"I hope so. By the way, I get the impression that you think your ideas have fallen on less-than-willing ears, either mine or those of the monks here. That's not the case, and I want you to know that. Brother Elwin came back to me after pondering the matter, and he said that he concurs about the autopsy. It's not a clear-cut case of natural causes, and we're better off being sure, especially if something did go amiss."

"Thank you, Abbot. But I still feel bad. Perhaps it's just that, after those recent deaths back home — deaths that I've considered unfair, to put it mildly — this death of Father James here hasn't helped matters much for me. That was, after all, the reason I came here on retreat. If this can get settled, it should go a long way toward helping Father Peter and me resolve the issues I've shared with him."

"Well, good luck with Peter. And know that I'll inform you about the autopsy when we get word." With that, the pair went to the eleven o'clock Mass.

Father John was glad to be able to talk during lunch and not have to listen to Thomas Merton but, as they were eating, he noticed that one of the monks pulled the abbot aside briefly. As they talked, the abbot's face indicated that he didn't like what he was hearing.

As the meal was ending, Abbot Mark asked Father John to walk with him back to the monastery. But the route chosen by the abbot was pointedly not the most direct. He walked out the end of the building nearest the church and away from the stream of monks heading back the other way to the monastery. Once he was certain they couldn't be overheard, the abbot said quietly: "Poison has been rumored by one or two of the monks. And the word is spreading rapidly, I'm told."

"Is there anything you can do to squelch that?" Father John asked.

"I don't think so. For one thing, anything I say now will probably sound like damage control — which, of course, it would be. But I mean that it wouldn't ring true. And they're mentioning Thurman, too."

"Maybe you could say something about doing things to rule out that awful possibility? Might you even tell them that you'll be seeing Mister Thurman?"

"Yes, to the first suggestion, but I don't think I'll mention Thurman. Not just yet, at any rate. He's in their thoughts already, and there's no need to pour gasoline on that fire."

"Do you think we were overheard when I mentioned it to you?"

"No, I don't. There was no one around. This is just the product of their natural curiosity, I believe. Or their creativity ... I'm not sure which. You probably remember what it was like when you were in the seminary. A closed environment like a seminary or a monastery means the inhabitants don't often have much of anything new to talk about. And, goodness knows, our monks here don't pay that much attention to outside news. So this sort of thing is wonderful grist for their mill."

"Is there anything you want me to do or say, Abbot?"

"No. Lay low, please. This theoretically doesn't involve you. But, as far as that goes, I hope it doesn't hinder your retreat with Father Peter."

"That should be the least of your concerns, Abbot. We'll do okay, I believe. And you certainly have far weightier things to deal with, anyway. But thanks for the thought."

"If you'll pardon me, then, I need to talk to the Prior and Sub-Prior," the abbot said as he went into the monastery. "See you later."

Father John chose to stay outside and turned back in the direction of the Guesthouse across from the Abbey church, to sit there on one of the benches under the trees. It was a very pleasant afternoon, and he intended to use the moment to digest the fast-paced string of events taking center stage in his mind.

A middle-aged monk appeared next to him suddenly and asked if he could sit with him.

"Certainly. Where'd you come from? I didn't see you approach."

He hadn't met this particular monk yet but could see that he seemed pleasant enough. Just from his greeting, he appeared to be a matter-of-fact kind of person.

"I didn't startle you, I hope. I was late getting out of lunch. I noticed you chatting with the abbot and didn't want to interrupt. Did he tell you what's being rumored?"

"What?" Father John said, feigning ignorance.

"That James might have been poisoned."

"You don't say." Father John managed a shocked look on his face.

"Well, you may not know, but there was a Brother here 'til recently who didn't like James. He was seen back here a few weeks after he left, and when some monks rumbled about not liking that, the abbot spoke to all of us to say that the visit was a sanctioned one between him and that former Brother. And he said we shouldn't be concerned and certainly shouldn't be speaking so uncharitably.

"That seemed to satisfy everyone ... until James' death yesterday. Now a couple of monks have become suspicious and have begun to speak out. They've gone so far as to suggest that our former confrere might have tried to hurt James, and that whatever he did may have gotten out of hand."

"That's very disturbing. But why are you mentioning this to me, Brother? I'm sorry, but I don't even know your name."

"Pardon me. I'm Brother Giovanni. I teach science here at the university: mostly chemistry, but one class in physics and some general science classes — introductory courses for freshmen. I shouldn't have assumed that you knew me or knew what I do here. Anyway, I thought you should know about this, lest you get swept up into it and not know what was going on. I hope I've not disturbed you. I know you're here on retreat, and that ought to be a quiet time for you."

"Well, the news is disturbing, but I wouldn't say that you've disturbed *me*. Not, at least, in the sense that you've disrupted my retreat. I guess I'm grateful to you. At least I'll understand now if conversations of that sort pop up."

"There is one other thing, Father. It's a piece of trivia, really, but because I'm in the sciences, it's of some interest to me. You may have heard the term 'monksbane' before. It's sometimes spelled as one word, sometimes as two, and it's supposedly a poison that was either discovered or developed by monastics in the Middle Ages."

"I'm not sure I ever heard that before, Brother."

"Well, it's a misused word, at any rate. It probably came about by confusing wolfsbane and monkshood. The proper term ought to be wolfsbane, in my opinion. But I think the misuse has crept into our language. Anyway, you may hear that term if these rumors reach you. One of the monks has mentioned it to me already today."

"Are you saying that the same substance might be called monksbane *or* wolfsbane?"

"Mistakenly so, but yes. Wolfsbane is a plant, and it *is* poisonous; monkshood is also a plant, but is not toxic. And people sometimes use the term 'monksbane' when they should be saying 'wolfsbane.' But, as I said, it's just a bit of trivia. Don't let it confuse you."

"Do you think Father James was poisoned, Brother? Perhaps even by wolfsbane?"

"I can't know for sure about either of those things, can I? But I don't *think* so. I don't think he was poisoned ... on purpose, that is. He wasn't *murdered*, is what I'm saying. And I highly doubt, therefore, that anything like wolfsbane was used. I wouldn't know where you'd get it, for one thing! And I *really* don't think the former Brother Oswald would do anything like that, in the first place. He didn't seem to like James, to be sure, but from what I knew of the man, he'd never do that, never go so far as to do bodily harm to him, let alone kill the man."

"Then you think Father James simply died of old age or a heart attack or something like that?"

"I suppose. But not by poison, for goodness sake!"

"And *monksbane* ... ?"

"Just an interesting coincidence, I suppose. Merely trivia. But I thought it interesting enough to bring it up, so long as I was giving you this warning."

"But an interesting coincidence, surely. A monk dies, and someone suspects something like monksbane. I'm intrigued, especially since I never heard the word before."

"Oh, it's been used. It's out there, as they say. But maybe you'd have to have a science background to have caught it."

"I'm intrigued enough that I might just try to research it. Though, I must say, I'm sorry that it took the death of one of your confreres to arouse my curiosity."

"If you find anything, let me know," Brother Giovanni said as he rose from the bench.

"I will. And thanks for the alert."

The monk waved genially as he walked toward the monastery.

Father John rose, too, and made his way directly to the library. *Might as well do a little searching while this is on my mind. It may also help take my mind off all these disturbing things.*

Well over an hour of investigation turned up very little, however. The Oxford English Dictionary turned out to be his best source, but even it didn't offer much that was satisfying. Nor did any scientific volumes verify the existence of a substance or plant named monksbane, no matter whether it was spelled as one word or two. The OED mentioned monkshood and wolfsbane, of course, and even offered some uses of the term monksbane, but it indicated that they weren't literally accurate.

When Father John decided that he was at a dead end, it still wasn't time for his appointment with Father Peter, so he returned to his bench outside the Guesthouse, making a mental note to tell Giovanni that his search had turned up nothing.

It continued to feel pleasant outdoors, and he sat enjoying the gentle breeze. He spent the remaining time before his appointment thinking about the curiosity of his being still attached to 'fairness' as the proper way to judge the events of life, despite the clear understanding to the contrary that was now in his mind. All he could come up with was that, having thought along those lines for so long, it had implanted itself so deeply that rooting it out now would take time. Or maybe it was something like thought versus emotion. He couldn't be sure.

When four o'clock came, he made his way upstairs to Father Peter. *I hope he's got a better handle on all my concerns than I have.*

CHAPTER XVIII

Outside Father Peter's door, he decided not to bring up the possibility of poison, even though it was out in the open now as far as he was concerned, thanks to Giovanni. He would concentrate on the fairness thing, instead. *That's what I'm here for, after all.*

After hearing an invitation to come in, he opened the door and greeted the old monk. "I hope you're feeling a bit more at peace today, Father."

"I am, yes, thank you. It took a while, but I think I'm okay with James' death now. Please sit. But let me open my window a bit more before we begin. The breeze seems very nice this afternoon."

"It is. I've been sitting outside most of the afternoon. But for all that time to think, I'm sorry to admit, I'm no farther along than the last time I was here."

"I apologize to you. I should have told you to reread the Genesis selections before you left the last time."

"Creation, you mean?"

"The creation of our first parents, at any rate ... but also their fall."

"You think the root of things for me lies in disobedience, Father?"

"No — something else, something subtly different. Let me reread for you that section of Genesis. Perhaps something will jump out at you."

Father John listened as the monk read the first several chapters of Genesis and marveled at how thoughtfully he read and how rich his voice sounded throughout.

When he had finished and looked up at his retreatant, Peter asked: "Anything else besides disobedience grab you just now?"

"Not really. Sorry."

"No need for apologies. Let's pick it apart, then. You realize this section is the Hebrew creation myth? In imitation of the pagans around them, they wrote their own story about creation that, like the other stories, reflects what they thought about their God. The pagans believed in good gods and bad, and their stories reflect the goodness in their world as coming from their good gods and the bad things, therefore, as coming from the bad ones.

"But the Hebrews believed in only one God, and a good God at that. Everything their God made was good, consequently. So first off, we see that they considered their whole world as good and everything in it, including humans.

"How explain evil, then? They needed the story of their first parents' fall to explain that bad gods didn't mess things up. Nor was it bad demigods, such as angels, although they seemed to have a minor role in things. Satan, the serpent, was a tempter, after all. But he was not responsible for introducing evil into the world. Adam and Eve did that.

"So far, I assume, I've told you nothing new."

"Right."

"Well, then, let's zero in on the actual sin of our first parents, as told in that Genesis story ... or myth. You don't have a problem with the term, 'myth,' do you?"

"No. I've learned that it doesn't mean something false but that it's, rather, a poetic explanation of something true — not *literally* true, mind you, but *metaphorically* ... sort of like Goldilocks and the three bears. Even little kids pick up on the fact that bears don't talk, eat oatmeal or sleep in beds. But that story's a wonderful way to teach children respect for other people's property. Far better than having them memorize 'thou shalt not steal.'"

"Correct. We're on the same page, then. Good! So that part of the Genesis myth is meant to explain how evil got into our world and, simply put, the Hebrew explanation is that it was our own fault. We humans did it, as symbolized by Adam and Eve.

"But that's where something often goes askew. Many people see the sin as disobedience, of course. But there's a problem when the interpretation of that leads to a simplistic, black-and-white understanding of God's Law and especially of the sanctions for it — that is, the punishments *and* rewards."

"It isn't disobedience?"

"It is, but that term alone doesn't explain everything we need to know about how God's Law — Natural Law — works *or* how its sanctions work, either. Therein, I think, lies an instructive truth or two that can help you with your 'fairness' problem."

"I hope so. But I have to say, it's still not clear."

"Not to worry. We'll keep taking it a piece at a time."

The monk went silent momentarily, and Father John thought he was about to ask a question. Instead, after some seconds, he went on with his explanation.

"It's a question of whether the sanctions are applied intrinsically or extrinsically. It matters whether God administers the punishment or whether it's a part and parcel of the sin, so to speak. Are you following me?"

"Keep going ... "

"Think about it. Gluttony's a good example. Why is it considered wrong — why does God say it's wrong? Because God just whimsically wants that, or because gluttony doesn't work for us humans?"

"Well, it certainly doesn't do a person any good. And if that's not clear in the short haul, it surely should be easy for even the dullest person to see in the long run."

"Right. Gluttony's wrong because it's intrinsically bad for people. And the 'punishment' is the damage it does to a person: physically and otherwise. In other words, the sin brings about its own punishment. God doesn't intervene or need to. Or, to put it another way, the punishment comes *intrinsically, not extrinsically.*"

"But then, why do we think of it as otherwise?" Father John asked. "Why do we insist on believing that it's God who deals out punishments?"

"I think it's because we tend to see God as like ourselves or, as scholars say, we anthropomorphize God. When we humans enact laws and exact punishments for breaking them, we can only punish in an extrinsic fashion. We *add* the punishment *on to* the crime — and administer it, by the way, only after the fact of catching people in a violation. It's the only thing we can do because we're not powerful enough or smart enough to be able to do it any other way, to do it the way God can. We can't build the punishment into the crime itself because we can't *create*.

"God, on the other hand, can make a world that self-corrects, so to speak. Violate something in God's creation, and creation itself will get you. The punishments are built in.

"The rewards are too, of course. The reason love is 'good' is that it's the only thing that really promotes the health and well-being of people — spiritually, mentally, emotionally, etc."

"I see that. But connect that again to 'fairness,' Father." Father John looked at the monk eagerly.

"If you insist on seeing the death of young Pete or that trucker as something bad — as a punishment — you'll only end in grief and confusion *if* you think such things happen because God acts outside the way his creation works.

"But if, instead, you understand that all things play out according to the way they're made — according to their nature — then, not only might you refrain from labeling such things as good or bad, but you'll especially understand that God doesn't impose them on us *in the wake of and because of* some action or another. God doesn't work the way we work: waiting for a violation of a law and then pouncing with some punishment. And, while we're at it, God doesn't sit around waiting to give out gold stars for behaving the right way, either.

"The rewards and the punishments are built in. They flow from the fact that God made us a certain way. When we behave consonant with that nature or make-up, we experience the end result as good. And when we don't do that, we experience the end result as bad.

"That's the truest and best way to understand how sin and virtue work. That's an insight we need to learn, by the way; we're not born realizing it. In fact, we should consider that piece of learning as one of the necessary steps in the spiritual maturation process."

"Are you saying that a view like mine is really spiritually immature?"

"That's one way to put it. But put that way, it probably sounds demeaning to an adult. Nonetheless, it's basically true. We just need to find a better, more palatable, way to express that, so people will want to keep growing spiritually."

He paused.

"You know, I've found that it's often when something traumatic occurs that people have the opportunity to push that growth forward. You've actually been given a blessing, Father. Those horrible acts have served as an invitation for your spirit to do some growing."

"And disobedience?"

"Oh, yes. The Genesis story! The real sin of Adam and Eve wasn't disobedience simply understood. It's much more subtle than that. The real issue, if you think about it, is that their disobedience amounted to trying to *play God*. They wanted to make their own rules!

"And, of course, that didn't work ... because they weren't capable of breaking away from the way they were made. They weren't able to remake even a part of their world in the way God made the whole of it. So when they violated the rules, God's rules, look what happened: their sin itself punished them.

"Well before God returns to them in the garden, they realize they're naked — something they experience as bad. They're ashamed and hide behind crude clothing. Actually, they've always been naked, but they had never before experienced it as bad or shameful. Only after their 'sin' does that awareness occur. And God doesn't do that to them. It just happens. Or, if you wish, the sin does that to them.

"Notice also that clothing hides them from each other — an interesting development, since they're man and wife, after all! But then they also hide from God in the garden — something silly on the surface of it, no? One can't hide from God, after all! All this hiding symbolizes the fact that they've become alienated from one another, as well as from God. And there's a further alienation: from nature — as symbolized by their need to exit the garden.

"When God finally shows up, the 'punishments' are not so much administered by him as *declared* by him. They're already in place. God didn't impose them."

"What about 'death?' God tells them they'll have to die, right?"

"Again, it's an announcement, not an imposition. Alienation — from each other, from God and from nature — *is* death. Adam and Eve just haven't stopped breathing yet. Their very makeup calls for connection to — not disconnection from — God, nature and other people. They've already begun to die in the most real sense of the word: their *spirit* is dying. Physical death, when it comes, will simply finalize the process. And, notice: death too was brought on by their sin, not by a vengeful or angry God."

"Tell me more about alienation being death."

"In a strange turn of events, when Adam and Eve tried to play God, they got their wish, after a fashion. They got to *be like God* — they got to be *alone.* I mean, before creation, there was just God. God was alone. Nothing else existed. We Christians believe in a triune God, and we can imagine the Father, Son and Spirit loving one another before creation. And we can understand that God needed nothing else than to be God — to be complete, so to speak.

"If you wish to be God, you are, in effect, wishing to be alone! The only problem was that, given the way they were made, our first parents couldn't handle being alone. They were made to connect, not disconnect. Their aloneness, their alienation, felt bad to them. And it was! It was a kind of death, death to their deepest selves, their very spirit."

Father John sat in silence almost a minute before saying: "I think I'm beginning to get it. But I'd like to pray over this some more. I mean, it's an awful lot all at once."

"Agreed. We'll have time tomorrow. The abbot hasn't announced the time for the funeral yet, so it can't possibly take place before Tuesday. Tomorrow, therefore, should work. Morning or afternoon?"

"That's up to you, Father."

"Late morning, then. Let's say 11. Okay?"

"Fine with me. And thank you *very much* for this. I think we've nearly come to the end of my concerns."

Father Peter was smiling as he watched his retreatant leave his room.

CHAPTER XIX

Father John didn't have a chance to talk with the abbot before the day ended. He stayed in the Abbey church a few minutes after Night Prayer and spent the time in the quiet church praying for Father James, even though he was fairly convinced that the old monk wasn't much in need of prayer. By the time he got to his room, he realized that further prayer about what he had discussed with Father Peter was called for too, and with those thoughts prayerfully occupying him, he lay in bed waiting for sleep before finally drifting off a few minutes later. When he awoke in the morning, he felt surprisingly refreshed and eager for the day ahead.

During Morning Prayer, he quickly found himself distracted, however, thinking about the monks at prayer around him. He had met a number of them, but the only ones that he knew somewhat well were Abbot Mark, Father Peter, and Brothers Michael and Bruno. His dealings with the others had been superficial, at best, so he began silently appraising them as they prayed.

Prior Raymond and Sub-Prior Jonathan were in their early sixties, if not older. Both struck him as men of serious demeanor, though he had already gotten a hint from the abbot that Jonathan did have a playful side. Both were of average height, and he found himself wondering what qualities had so impressed the abbot that he would choose them for the number two and three slots in the monastery's hierarchy. Barely realizing that he was doing it, he ruled them out as suspects in Father James' death.

Good grief! Of course they're above suspicion! But then, if Father James was done in, perhaps not all the monks should be automatically considered innocent. With that, his initially casual perusal of the monks in the church took on a more careful, if not sinister, tone.

The younger monks, who sat in the first row on each side of the assembly as they chanted the Office, looked innocent enough, but that was probably a prejudice stemming from their youthful looks. That was certainly true of the newest community members, who not only looked young but were: Nathanael, Bruno, Justin and Thomas, as well as the two seminarians, Julian and Michael. Brothers Martin, Dominic and Donald, while a few years older, still qualified as young, at least in contrast to the remaining members of the community.

Those youngsters were a motley crew physically. Most were notably slim, several above average in height, and only one, Donald, slightly built and short. They were an appealing lot, good-looking and outgoing, at least so far as he could determine from having watched them at several Haustus moments. Aside from those visual impressions, however, Father John had to admit that he didn't have much else to go on for those young monks.

He had a bit more knowledge about a few of the other monks, the 'older' ones. He knew Robert to be a gentle and simple soul and, as such, well above suspicion. Elwin too was no suspect. His genuine and well-displayed concern for the whole community had already impressed Father John. And what he knew about the oldest of the monks, Peter, William and former Abbot Innocent, certainly raised them above suspicion.

But as he looked over the rest of the monks that morning, he knew that the best he could manage was vague impressions. And that, he knew, came nowhere near removing them from any list of potential suspects.

By the time he came to that conclusion, Morning Prayer was at an end, and it was time to leave for breakfast. Ashamed that he had wasted a precious chance to pray for the church and the world, Father John promised silently to do better in the opportunities for formal prayer that remained for him at St. Martin's.

All he had to show for his distractions that morning, thus, was a rather small number of monks that he could exclude from a list of suspects. He again hoped that the autopsy scheduled for that day would rule out poison, but if it did not show that, then what? He didn't like any of the remaining possibilities. Breakfast proved a welcome, if temporary, respite for him.

On his way back across the street afterward, he walked out of the dining hall with Brother Hilary. "What's your job here, Brother? Or should I have put that some other way?"

Hilary was a short, spare man in his fifties, as far as Father John could tell. He had a high forehead and a graying crown of hair around a large bald spot on the very top of his head, and his eyes sparkled as he talked.

"No. That's fine. My 'job' is to teach French and Latin at our university, but you probably also saw me leading song. Besides teaching, I'm the monastery's cantor."

"Weren't there others singing with you at Mass yesterday?"

"Yes. Brother Thomas, one of our youngest and newest members, helps with the singing. And, of course, Father Justus is also with us, besides playing the organ. We might soon be breaking in one other of the monks, too."

"Yes. I met Justus last week, and he told me he teaches here, too. I guess a number of you wear more than one hat."

"That's typical in a monastery."

"Now that you mention it, that was also true at Meinrad's when I studied there eons ago."

"So," the monk said, "is your retreat here going well?"

"I'm having what may well be my final session with Father Peter in a little over an hour. And, yes, it's going well — particularly the last couple of times we spoke."

"Father Peter's a darling. Even some time back, when he was still teaching, that was true. I took literature from him when I came to the monastery. Many of us monks studied here, I suppose you know — usually during our earliest years. Peter made literature, particularly American literature, very interesting for our class — fun, too."

"The tons of books in his room certainly attest to his love of that. Although, to be honest, he has a lot of books on other subjects."

"Some of us have accused him of being addicted to reading." Hilary chuckled quietly. "He has *always* liked to read."

"By the way, may I inquire how you got your name? Hilary isn't exactly a household word."

"Just before our first vows, each of us gets to submit a small list of names we'd prefer. The abbot at the time — Father Innocent — didn't act very *innocently* with regard to my list, I'm afraid. Hilary wasn't one of my choices. But he seemed to get no small delight out of assigning that name to me. Over the years, I've gotten used to it. But way back then, I would rather have had some variant on the root 'Colum' — Columbanus, Columkill, Columba — something like that. I was pretty much into my Irish heritage at the time. By now, though, it's not a big deal. Hilary works. And, for all I know, not getting any of my choices might have been good for my humility!" He chuckled again, this time more audibly.

"It, of course, comes from the Latin root for laughter. And there are some monks here who claim that I'm well-named. And that satisfies me." His cheeks turned rosy and he chuckled again, this time rather loudly.

They had by that time arrived at the door to the monastery nearest the Abbey church. "Before you get away, Brother, have you heard anything about Father James' funeral? Has the time been announced?"

"Ordinarily we have funerals at 10 or 11 in the morning, but there's been no announcement yet as to which day. I doubt if they'll be able to have it before Wednesday. There are too many people to be contacted. My guess is that we'll bury James on Wednesday … Thursday at the latest. But I'm sure the abbot will get the word out, once everything's decided."

"I'll wait to hear, then. Nice talking with you, Brother," Father John said, as the monk stepped inside the monastery.

Scratch off one more monk from the list of suspects, Father John mused as he stood outside the monastery. *Hilary doesn't seem likely.*

He looked at his watch. *Too soon to be knocking on Father Peter's door — I've still got over an hour to kill. Wonder how to occupy myself 'til then. Perhaps someone's in the campus ministry office.*

He ambled over to the far end of the main building, ascended the stairs to the first floor, turned left inside and walked the several steps to the end of the building. Not only was no one there, but the door to the campus ministry offices was also locked. He did an about-face and wandered down the hall to the center of the building, encountering no one on the way. *Must be too early of a summer morning to find anyone stirring. Guess I'll go back to my room.*

He walked down the stairs in the center of the building's long wing, stepped outside and started across to the monastery. He waved at Brother Jude, who was pulling up to the front of the main building in his van. Jude was the campus postmaster and delivered mail, as well as departmental memos, all over campus. He looked quite fit, probably a result of all the walking he had to do.

By the time he got to the abbot's entrance of the monastery, the one nearest his own room, he had passed two of the monks on their way to the main building. Father Richard was probably headed toward food service to deal with some issue or another concerning the monastery dining room. Refectorian didn't strike Father John as a very stressful position, but there might be more than was apparent to being liaison between the monks and the university's kitchen. Father Simon, the abbey archivist and second monk that he passed, was probably en route to his computer in the main building. Father John couldn't imagine what else would bring him out of the monastery at that time of day.

He was soon in his room and reviewing his thoughts before seeing Father Peter. Within a few minutes he was pretty sure what he wanted to tell his retreat master, so he shifted his thinking to Father James. *If Wednesday is the day of his funeral, that will only give me Thursday in which to see Seattle ... if I can find a ride, that is. Of course, there's also the issue of* how *the old man died. Whatever that autopsy finds, I hope the abbot is satisfied that there was no foul play.*

Soon enough it was time to leave, and he made his way up the stairs, instead of using the elevator, having decided that the exercise would do him good. When he knocked on Father Peter's door a full five minutes early, he was happy to hear a cheery invitation to enter.

"Have you put things together in a fashion satisfactory to your spiritual comfort, Father?" Peter seemed relaxed.

"I think so. But, if I may, let me first tell you a bit more about myself." Father John felt relaxed, too, for the first time in many weeks.

"I've never been what you could call bookish, Father. I scraped by in the seminary, and it never bothered me that others were academically my betters. I never had aspirations to do great things theologically, nor dreamt that I would — or should — be called to anything more important than parish work. I have what even I would call a simple faith and have always believed that in some strange way that simple faith qualified me — and in the very best of ways, in my opinion — to do good work in any parish to which the bishop might send me. Over the years, I've gloried in all the parish work that I was given. With all that in mind, I'm sure you can understand that I never got very deeply into the whys and wherefores of faith. I took it, and how it worked, pretty much for granted, even while understanding many things that might undermine it for members of the flocks I've served in my time.

"But when this blue funk took hold of me recently, it really knocked me off my feet. Somehow I never dreamed something like that would come to roost on *my* shoulders. As I saw it, that sort of thing would only happen to my parishioners and, more than likely, only to a few of them.

"So you can't believe how grateful I am that you've been able to help me with this. And I'm grateful for the way you've done it: so gently and non-judgmentally. You've slowly and methodically taken me through steps that help — on more than one level — and I even understand now how I could have been something of a sitting duck for this spiritual low point. And I think I also know — thanks to you — how to get back my spiritual balance — and keep it.

"So, for all this, I'm most grateful. And I don't want our moments together to go any farther before being sure you hear that gratitude."

"All in a day's work, Father … as I suspect, from your own pastoral experience, you already know." The monk was grinning broadly.

"Yes, but as to the particulars, the only clarification I would still like, Father Peter, concerns what I'll call free will. If I've understood what you said, I believe a bit more can be highlighted about that to make it clearer for me. You convinced me that God isn't directly — extrinsically — behind any sanctions for either good or bad deeds. But I think that concept includes the element of our freedom to make choices."

"Yes ... " Father Peter began hesitantly. "Of course, we are free to make any and all choices. But I thought your main concern was whether it was God who was directly responsible for the things we construe as punishments, like those deaths in your hometown."

"True. But it tacks it all down for me with complete finality when I understand that not only are the rewards and punishments built in to the actions we choose, but also that our very choices themselves are in no way influenced by God ... that they are, in fact, totally and utterly freely made. The inclusion of free will makes it completely clear that we have absolutely no one to blame but ourselves for the consequences of all our actions.

"But after that insight, I then realized there was yet *one other* loose end: my sorrow at losing people close to me. I can usually deal with sadness such as that. But I got befuddled this time by mixing in God's 'interference.' Once you clarified that for me, all I had to do was figure out what was really bugging me deep down underneath everything. When I realized that it was my feeling sad about losing people important to me, I finally felt freed up from my spiritual depression.

"So, for all you've done to help me through this, Father Peter, I want to be sure you know how deeply thankful I am." Father John finally sat back and took a satisfied breath.

"I feel good to see you back on an even keel, Father John. All I ask as we conclude, then, is that you keep me in your prayers."

"Goes without saying, Father! You'll be in my prayers every day from now on."

"So now what? Will you be going back to Illinois immediately?"

"My ticket's set for Friday, so I will stick around for Father James' funeral. But, as I understand it, the time for that hasn't been announced yet."

"I think you're right about that. I've heard nothing, at any rate," Father Peter said.

"I'll see you around here for the next few days, then. And thanks again ... very much." Father John rose, shook Father Peter's hand and stepped lightheartedly into the second-floor corridor.

CHAPTER XX

When the abbot did not pull him aside after the noon meal, Father John figured that the autopsy results must not be available yet. On his way to his room, he decided to take care of his dirty laundry. Accordingly, he got his clothes and went directly to the laundry on the lowest floor of the monastery and across the hall from the community room.

As he was putting his laundry into two of the five washing machines there, Brother Robert came in with a shopping cart full of albs from the monastery church and greeted Father John. He seemed to be in fine spirits.

"Hello," Father John said. "Getting those here must have been a chore, Brother, given your cane and all."

"Not really. I keep this cart here in the laundry room and, when some albs need washing, I put it on the elevator and make my way to the church for as many of those vestments as I can carry. It usually takes a while, especially if I have to make more than one trip, but God knows I have plenty of time, so it's no big deal. And now that Father Gilbert has fixed up the room next to the exit into the slype as a sacristy, I have less distance to travel for the albs that are kept there."

"The *what*? Slype?"

"Slype, yes — the corridor from the abbey to the church."

"I never heard that word before, Brother. How is it spelled?"

"Just like you'd think, but with a 'y' instead of an 'i.' Truth to tell, I only learned the word lately ... from Brother Hilary. He thinks it's of either Welsh or British origin. But when I looked it up in the library, the dictionary said it might come from Flemish. It seems to date from medieval times, though, because that dictionary defined it as a covered walkway connecting a church with a chapter house. You know: a house that might be used by a chapter of canons, like at a medieval cathedral! I kind of like the word, actually. Not many of my confreres seem to know about it, so it's a great conversation piece."

"I'll be sure to keep it as part of my Benedictine trivia trove," Father John said, grinning. "But, anyway, it's your job to make sure all the albs are clean?"

"It's not an official position here at the abbey, if that's what you mean. But I volunteered to do it some time ago, and ever since — going on ten years now — I've kept us in clean albs. We could probably have trusted most individuals to make sure their own albs were nice-looking, but even if we did that, there are lots of other albs — for visitors, various ministers at Mass, and such — and those would probably not get cleaned that often if we didn't have a system for it. And I guess I'm that system. So I do *all* the albs. You're getting your own laundry squared away, I see, Father."

"Yes, though I didn't even think about it 'til last night. I hadn't planned to stay quite this long, you see, and it finally dawned on me that I don't have enough clothes for any extra time here. I'm glad this facility's available. And I'm glad it's also so easy to use."

"With this many people, we not only need a laundry, but one with this many machines."

"By the way, are my washers hogging space you need for the albs?"

"Oh, certainly not. There's plenty of room in the other three washers for what I've got today. But even if that weren't the case, I could leave the albs here and do them later today. No problem at all, Father. I've got plenty of time, as I said, and we don't even need these vestments immediately. So you can just keep on doing what you're doing."

"Good. What besides cleaning these albs will be occupying your time today, then, Brother?"

"Just some personal things. What about you, Father?"

"As a matter of fact, I've finished seeing Father Peter, so nothing's pressing for me right now. Although, I'm curious as to when Father James' funeral will be held. Have you heard anything?"

"No, I haven't."

"Any guesses?"

"Wednesday's a good possibility."

"Thanks. That's what some of the other monks thought."

Brother Robert put his load into two of the remaining machines and was soon out of the laundry room. After Father John had put his clothes into a dryer, he decided to go to his room for a book to read while he waited for them to finish. Within forty-five minutes, he had gathered his clothes and was returning to his room with them held warmly against his chest.

As he got off the elevator on the floor above, he saw the abbot's open door and popped his head inside to ask about the autopsy.

"Yes, I have the report. You might want to put your clothes away and come back," the abbot said.

Father John dumped everything onto his bed, and when he had returned, Abbot Mark asked him to close the door behind him. "Please sit over here, Father," the abbot said, gesturing toward a corner of his room where several chairs and a sofa formed a comfortable discussion area.

When they had settled in, the abbot said: "Let me tell you first that I saw Herb Thurman in town this morning, and I'm satisfied that when he returned here the other day, the only thing he did was see me. He said he didn't visit with Father James in his room or anywhere else, nor did he go elsewhere in our monastery other than my quarters. I believe him and, as far as I am concerned, that rules him out as a suspect in any kind of foul play."

"Did the autopsy indicate foul play, Abbot?"

"Not on the surface of things, no. What it found was that Father James died of anaphylactic shock. He choked to death, Father."

"Anaphylactic shock? Like a diabetic coma?"

"*Like* that, yes. But in his case, it was caused by his allergy to peanuts."

"I guess you're relieved that it wasn't poison, then?"

"Yes. But now we have a new problem."

"What would that be? I don't follow."

"Our own questioning of the monks indicated that peanuts or peanut products could not have been involved."

"What are you saying, Abbot?" The relief that he had begun to feel was suddenly eroded.

"I'm saying that we can't figure out how James' allergy was triggered. So we're not at all out of the woods ... because the only thing making sense at this time is that someone did this to him, and we can't rule out that it was done deliberately."

CHAPTER XXI

The slightest of smiles was playing across the abbot's face.

"I don't see what's so funny, Abbot," Father John said. "I had hoped that it wouldn't be poison, and now this seems to be as bad."

"This situation surely isn't, but your face just now was. You may not have realized it, but your jaw dropped noticeably a moment ago."

"I guess it could have. You certainly caught me off-guard with what you said. How can you be so sure that peanuts weren't somehow involved — in somewhat less diabolical a fashion, perhaps, but involved, nonetheless?"

"For one thing, there are no nuts of any kind in the snack bar, and Father James was deliberately kept in the dark about where we hid the peanut butter. He was short enough that he'd have to use a step stool to reach it, and given his age, that was problematic. Besides, he knew enough to avoid anything that could trigger a reaction. His Alzheimer's hadn't progressed far enough for us to worry about him in that regard. And I can assure you that, besides all this, we have kept a close watch on him. Something set his allergy off, all right, and it had to be nuts in some form or another. But there doesn't seem to be a way for that to have happened. And that leaves open the possibility of foul play.

"When the Prior questioned everyone in the monastery, the answers he received convinced him that, as far as we all were concerned, no nuts in any form had been available to James in that room. *As far as we can determine,* then, nothing that any of us did has contributed to James' seizure and death.

"So you conclude that we have a mystery here?"

"I'm saying that we can't figure out how that allergic reaction happened. So we're just as stymied as if poison were involved. We're simply unable to exclude the possibility that someone did him in. As unwilling as I am to truly believe that happened, it hasn't been ruled out."

"We can still hope that it was an accident ... tragic, but an accident — can't we?" Father John felt himself hoping against hope.

"Whatever! But I believe we have to get to the bottom of this, Father."

"Will you be able to bury him before you do figure it out?"

"I'm not sure. We may have to talk to the police first ... unless, of course, we can get this thing figured out soon. Thank goodness he has no close relatives nearby. The few that he has aren't sure they can come, given the distance — they all live in Idaho — though they asked to be informed once we set the date."

"I don't wish to appear forward, but I'll be glad to assist in any way I can. Father Peter and I have finished our discussions — successfully, I'm happy to say — and I have plenty of time now. I won't be leaving 'til Friday morning."

"What makes you think that you could possibly help, Father?" Abbot Mark said, with a slight frown on his face.

"Well, for one thing, didn't you say that it was a small handful of monks who used the snack bar before Father James died?"

"That's what Father Raymond determined, yes."

"I imagine you'll be wanting to talk to the community again, just to be sure all possibilities can be clearly ruled out, won't you? I mean: some small lack of clarity in the previous questions or answers could surface in a second round of questioning, mightn't it?"

"Possibly."

"Well, during that second questioning of your community, I'd be glad to sit with the Prior. An objective outsider like me could maybe catch something that members of the community might otherwise miss, no?"

"You may have a point. It certainly couldn't hurt. Let me call Father Raymond. The three of us can brainstorm this."

"If you don't mind, I'll go back to my room and sort my clothes. The two of you may wish to talk alone, anyway. When I'm finished, I'll just wait outside 'til you're ready for me."

"Thoughtful of you, Father. Let's do that."

Father John soon returned and had only several minutes to wait before the abbot's door opened for him.

"You've already met Father Raymond, have you not, Father?" The abbot was standing in front of his desk as he acknowledged the Prior at his side.

"Yes, thank you."

The three men sat down in the same corner of the abbot's quarters that Father John had just vacated. "I've told our Prior here what you said, Father, and he agrees that it's not a bad idea. Let's talk more about it, though." The abbot was looking more relaxed than Father John had anticipated. "But before that, would you like something to drink? Coffee, water, soda ... anything?"

"No, I'm all right." Father John said.

"To start with, may I clarify something for you, Father Raymond?"

"Surely."

"Back in my home parish over the past twelve months, there have been a mysterious death and numerous crimes that I got pastorally involved with. Just so you know, therefore, I'm no stranger to the sort of thing that we have here, even though I'll be quick to admit that I'm no expert ... just somewhat experienced.

"That said, it's my understanding that you checked with every member of the community in residence here as to whether they did anything with food in the snack bar over the twenty-four hours — maybe even forty-eight hours — before Father James died. Did I hear that correctly?"

"Yes. That's what I did. Forty-eight hours! I even received something about that from you. I talked to *everyone* who was known to be here at the time."

"Right. Did you do that more or less informally, or was there a precise set of questions that you asked each person? As I recall, it sounded pretty casual when I was asked by the abbot."

"I'd have to say that it was an informal procedure," Raymond said as the abbot nodded.

"Then may I suggest that we work out a more formal set of questions to now use with each member of your community?"

"That's probably a good idea," the abbot said.

Within ten minutes the three were satisfied with what they had put together, and Father Raymond suggested: "Why don't the three of us answer these questions here and now."

They quickly determined that Father John hadn't even known where the room was and was certainly not in it before James died, and also that neither the abbot nor Father Raymond had used the snack bar during the time in question.

"That leaves thirty-four more of us, then," the abbot said. "Do you want to see who's here in the house right now and get started with them, Raymond?"

Father John spoke up quickly. "Might it not be better to set it up in such a way that Father Raymond and I could see everyone in one short period? Perhaps tonight after supper?"

"Why do it that way?" the abbot wanted to know.

"It's the most objective way, I believe, and it rules out the possibility of accidental — and, especially, deliberate — collusion. If we can get all the monks into one room and keep them there while we question them one at a time in a second room, we stand the best chance of getting the truth about this. I'm not accusing anyone, mind you, but if you want to be sure of learning what happened, I think this allows us to fully rule out anything worrisome on the part of your monks ... or pinpoint something nefarious, if such be the case."

"You're proposing, Father, that we keep the monks from talking to one another before we question each of them, is that right?" Father Raymond asked.

"Correct. If, indeed, only a handful dealt with food in the snack bar the day or two before James died, we should be able to dismiss the bulk of the monks quickly. And with them out of the way, so to speak, talking to the few who had the capability of contributing in some way to his death shouldn't take all that long."

"I agree with that, Father Abbot," Father Raymond said.

Father John continued. "The other thing I think we should be sure of is this: will everyone in the monastery be at supper? If so, an announcement of what we're doing can be made then. After that, we have to get them all into one room together. We also need to be sure that they don't leave there until we've had a chance to talk to each of them separately. Oh yes: they also can't go back to the first room until everyone has been talked to. Is all that possible?"

"Yes, everyone's here — no one's away from the monastery. And I can make a head count at supper to be sure they're present for the meal, so we do this properly," the abbot said. "Furthermore, I think I'll only announce at supper that I want to see all of them immediately in the community room. Everything else can be said to them there. That way, there'll be no talking among themselves about this on the way back to the monastery."

"Then where do we do this?" Father John asked. "I mean, if we put them all in the community room, what other room will we use for the questioning? And where do they go after being questioned?"

"We'll keep them in the community room, and Father John and I can see them individually in the chapter room," Father Raymond proposed. "And afterward we can have them go directly to chapel to pray for James. If we question Jonathan first, he can stand outside the chapter room and make sure they go directly to the church afterward."

"That should work," the abbot said.

"It goes without saying, Abbot," Father John volunteered, "that you need to reassure them about why I'll be involved. They should know that I'm just an outside observer listening for something you all might otherwise overlook. I also think, in line with that, that I shouldn't have anything to say while you deal with them, Father Raymond. Wouldn't you both agree?"

"Definitely as to both points, Father," the abbot said as the Prior nodded. "Raymond, you alone should ask the questions, and I will be sure to make that clear when I explain all this after supper."

Father Raymond spoke up. "I think it would be best not to have talking at supper tonight, as usual. No need to alter our routine and possibly arouse suspicion. And when you speak to them in the community room, Abbot, don't you think it might also be the best time to tell them about the autopsy?"

"Yes. That's what we'll do."

"I just thought of another thing," Father John said. "What if I catch something during the questioning? Should I speak up then?"

The three of them decided that in that event — and in that event only — Father John might speak, but that he should do so quietly to Father Raymond and allow him to pursue whatever seemed called for.

The process had taken the better part of an hour. Afterward, Father John returned to his own room across the hall from the abbot's office. His mind was abuzz with thoughts of everything they had just discussed. *I'd better think this out thoroughly, in case something else occurs to me before supper. And I think I'll skip Haustus before supper, lest I let something slip and botch this up.*

CHAPTER XXII

After supper, Father John went directly to the chapter room and waited there while the abbot spoke to all the monks in the community room down the hall. Soon after the abbot's voice went silent, Fathers Raymond and Jonathan joined him. The Sub-Prior was one of those who had not used the snack bar in the two crucial days in question, and Father Raymond was, accordingly, very quickly finished with him. Jonathan then took up his station in the corridor, agreeing to summon each monk from the community room and to tell each monk as he came out of the chapter room to go directly to the Abbey church.

It soon became apparent to Father John that the abbot was first sending all those monks who had not used the snack bar for any food. The vast majority of the monastery's inhabitants, therefore, were processed in short order.

The eight remaining members of the monastery were equally divided between younger and older men. Brothers Nathanael, Julian and Michael, among the young ones, had not eaten anything with nuts, and Brothers Basil, Anselm and Jerome, among the older monks, hadn't either. But Brothers Thomas and Frederick had made peanut butter sandwiches.

It was quickly determined that Frederick not only made his sandwich the day before James died but had insisted that he cleaned up after himself, putting all his dishes and utensils away after washing them. Father William had earlier said that he had cleaned up the snack bar at the end of the day before James died because it was his custom to do so each evening before he went to bed. Frederick was thus fully removed from suspicion of any possible complicity in James' death, deliberate or otherwise.

That left young Brother Thomas who, though he used the room on the morning of James' last day alive, insisted that he had also cleaned up after himself. The careful scrutiny of the snack bar after James' death clearly showed the peanut butter to be in its assigned hiding place, and with Thomas' assertion that he had taken the precautions that had been explained to them all, the mystery seemed nowhere nearer a solution by the end of that evening's session in the chapter room.

By the time the last monk had been questioned, it was time for Night Prayer, and only after that did the abbot, John and Raymond gather again in the Abbot's office to mull over the fruits of their labors.

"We seem to be back at square one, don't we?" the abbot said, a dejected look on his face.

Father John spoke up. "Let's just be sure we all agree on what we do and do not know."

But another five minutes of comparing notes only brought them back to the abbot's square one.

"Don't despair," Father John said. "We know *something* did Father James in, and we know it must have had something to do with nuts. There's got to be an explanation, however elusive it seems to be right now. Let's just pray that it's not something evil. I so want to believe it was an accident." But his words didn't seem to brighten the spirits of the other two. "We can sleep on it, surely?" he asked the abbot.

"We'll have to, won't we?"

"But," Father John persisted, "what about James' burial?"

"What about it?" the abbot asked.

"You had said that you might feel the need to call the police before deciding on a time for it. At least, that's what I remember, Abbot ... that, or words to that effect."

"Yes, I did indicate that."

"Well, it seems to me that you needn't involve the police right now, even if you decide that you want to bring them into this at a later date. Because you have the autopsy results *as well as* tonight's questioning of the entire monastery, both of which can be easily documented for a court, if need be. I'm of the opinion that you can proceed with his burial." He looked expectantly at the abbot.

Raymond chimed in, agreeing with Father John, though he made his assertion rather quietly.

The abbot finally spoke. "I'm in agreement with you both. We should set the funeral for Thursday, then, and even though I think James' relatives probably won't be joining us, I'll let them know tomorrow, just in case any of them wants to come over from Idaho. It's much too late to call tonight.

"That gives us two days to make all the preparations here. The funeral home already has James' body, and they can embalm him tomorrow, once I give the go-ahead. I had asked them to wait with that until tomorrow, anyway. James can be back here by tomorrow evening, and we can place his body in the church and leave it there throughout Wednesday for an extended wake. I think ten o'clock should work for the funeral on Thursday, wouldn't you agree, Father Raymond?"

Raymond nodded.

"Settled then, at least as far as the funeral is concerned. Raymond, will you please see to all the details here within the house? I'll put a notice on the bulletin board tonight." As Raymond was nodding, Abbot Mark continued. "I'll contact the funeral home first thing tomorrow, then. And I hope you both won't mind seeing me before Noon Prayer tomorrow, just in case something new has turned up."

Raymond and John agreed and, seconds later, both men were leaving the abbot's quarters.

It was a restless night for Father John, as he drifted in and out of sleep, his mind on the perplexing details surrounding James' death.

CHAPTER XXIII

Father John ate very little the next morning and was soon on his way back to his room after breakfast. As he stepped outside, he happened to pair up with Father Olav, a philosophy professor at St. Martin's.

"You saw the note on the board about Father James' funeral, I suppose?" the monk asked. He was a tall, slender and handsome man in his fifties, whose dark eyes looked out from deep sockets, his face thus projecting an overall intensity that was underscored by his deep voice and slow, deliberate manner of speaking.

"Yes," Father John answered. He saw no need to explain that he was already in possession of that information as of last night. "Didn't it say something about his body being in the Abbey church until the funeral?"

"Yes … our custom here," the monk said laconically.

"How does that work? Will there be someone with the body the whole time?"

Father Olav seemed to roll the question around in his mind before answering. "Yes. Teams of two monks each will spell each other kneeling in prayer for thirty-minute shifts. Once the church is locked after Night Prayer, however, the body will be left alone overnight. The grave has already been dug, by the way." The intense seriousness of his visage had not relaxed one whit.

"Where? Do you have a cemetery here on the property? Most monastic communities do, I would think."

"Yes," he said. As he continued, Father John got the distinct impression that the man's 'teacher voice' had now emerged. "When you come up the hill from the College Street entrance to our property, the road splits. Perhaps you noticed. The path to the left continues on past our cemetery and farther still to the buildings we used when we had a high school here. It's blocked off most of the time now by a metal gate, but that will be open, of course, on Thursday. You've not been back there?" The question had the ring of challenge to it.

"No. But now that I know about it, I might go there today. You said the grave's been dug already?"

"Yes. Several of the younger monks were given that task the day James died, not only because they have more energy for that kind of heavy work than the rest of us, but also to introduce them into the mystery and meaning of death for Benedictines. They were actually quite eager to do it. I think that was due mainly to the esteem in which they held James." He seemed surprised at those attitudes on the part of his young confreres.

"That's touching, actually," Father John said softly, as much to himself as to Father Olav. Somewhat louder, he asked, in an attempt to change the subject: "Do you think it will be a big funeral?"

"Probably not." The professorial tone was back. "James was old and came originally from Idaho — one reason, by the way, that he was posted back there as a pastor for a number of years. Anyway, I doubt many of his relatives will be coming from that far away. And, while some of our monks who are assigned outside the monastery will probably be with us here that day, the Archbishop probably won't come. So it will mostly be our community and perhaps a sprinkling of others in attendance ... not a very large crowd, therefore, is my guess."

"Well, I'm glad I have extended my stay. I'll be present, and gladly. I rather liked James, even though I only knew him for a few days."

The two fell silent for a time as they walked along, but Olav spoke up again when they reached the monastery, allowing a bit of self-disclosure to slip past his usual control. "I'm rather glad, myself, that the youngsters had to dig that grave."

"How so?"

His words came even more slowly and deliberately now. "They can be a pain at times, and that digging rather puts them in their place."

"Really?" Father John had no idea what had prompted that.

"Yes. They're a rather liberal crowd, you know. They fit quite well here on the left coast."

"*Left* coast?"

"Never heard that before?" Again, it was the professor showing through in his voice. "It refers to the left-leaning tendencies all up and down our country's west coast. California certainly and Washington, at least on our side of the mountains ... though it may be less true of Oregon."

"Oh, you mean politics ... the politics of the newer men?"

"Yes, but other things too," he said, warming to the topic. "They all have radios in their cells, and when you walk down the halls of the monastery, you can hear them listening to National Public Radio all the time. The jazz isn't so bad, I suppose, but I find the talk on those stations tiresome. And have you ever heard the names of the on-air people? Only in Washington!" He was speaking faster now, obviously relishing the opportunity to discuss something he felt deeply about.

"I hope I don't offend you, Father, but I listen to NPR in the Midwest myself, at least in the mornings." Father John was watching the man's face carefully. "I like to wake up to the news.

"But I know what you mean about the names. Some of them sound pretty strange. I mean, there are two guys on the morning news show with names that sound a little weird but also a lot alike: Inskeep and Ydstie. And there are lots of others that certainly sound foreign. One, I know, *is* a foreign correspondent: Sylvia Poggioli. But I've often wondered about the rest of them. Saraya Sarhaddi Nelson, comes to mind — sounds like she married a Brit or an American, but she surely must have come originally from India or some place like that, given that name of hers. And there's also Lakshmi Singh. I find all such names curious, all right. But it seems that the news is reported fairly and accurately, as far as that all goes."

"Perhaps," he conceded, "but the names I was referring to as strange are those of some of our local people. They're all women, by the way: Robin and Paige and Kirsten ... whose last name is Kendrick, by the way: Kirsten Kendrick!" There was no mistaking the dislike in his voice.

"Like the seminary in St. Louis?"

"No. There's a 'D' in her name: Kirsten *Kendrick.*" He enunciated the words slowly and overly distinctly, his impatience undisguised. "But the one that gets me most is Bellamy."

"Any relation to the actor? I liked him — Ralph Bellamy — especially in his portrayal of Roosevelt in 'Sunrise at Campobello.'"

"No relation that I know of. Bellamy's her *first* name." Father John couldn't help feeling that Olav was barely tolerating him at that moment for being more than a bit dense. "Her last name's equally interesting, by the way: Pailthorp. And there's also Sprince Arbogast. Where *do* they find these people?"

"I suppose I agree about those names. I can't imagine parents in the Midwest giving any of their children names like that."

That seemed to calm the monk some. But with barely a pause for breath, his voice regained its former intensity. "And furthermore, our young monks aren't all that tidy, either."

"What do you mean?"

"Unless they're specifically tasked with keeping some area clean, they seem not to notice messes anywhere, let alone help straighten them up. We were always encouraged — in fact, expected — to keep the community room presentable, for instance. And most of us still pitch in to do that even after all these years. But I've *never* seen them lifting a hand with that. And the snack bar! They've got to be reminded all the time to pick up after themselves there." It seemed to Father John that the monk was very near to anger.

"Funny you should mention that," Father John said, in an attempt to mollify Olav or at least somehow rein in the man's ire. "Why, just last night, several of them told Father Raymond that they *had* cleaned up after themselves in there before James died."

"Well, their idea of 'cleaning up,' doesn't always match that of us older monks, I can tell you."

Father John would have liked to change the direction of the conversation but didn't know how. "Like what?"

"It should be no trouble at all for them to clean their dishes when they've finished and put them away, but most of the time they *might* rinse them and put them beside the sink ... that is, when they don't just leave them dirty on the sideboard or in the sink itself." Olav had the look of a man who had just played a trump card.

Father John was silent, not knowing exactly how to respond. Reacting to his silence, Father Olav turned suddenly apologetic and said: "You must pardon me. I get off on this every so often." His voice and his visage had done an about-face. "I may have exaggerated a bit. But these things do get to me, as you can tell. It's nice to be able to vent my feelings every once in a while. I hope I haven't bored or offended you."

"Not to worry, Father. I have to admit that the young guys back in my diocese certainly strike us older fellows as ... well, different, shall we say?" Glad to have the conversation end amicably, he smiled at the monk.

Father Olav nodded and stepped into the monastery, leaving Father John of a mind to turn on his heel and go in search of the cemetery.

He walked down the hill toward the split in the road. *It's got to be hard to gather a group of people together, especially one of varying ages, and not find some points of difference like that. Perhaps such things mostly go unspoken at this abbey ... I haven't noticed anything disagreeable erupting into the open before, at any rate.*

Although, perhaps none of the monks would want to display anything like that in front of a stranger like me.

He reached the cemetery and promptly put aside his conversation with Olav to look at the headstones and pray for the monks buried there. And, of course, James' open grave could hardly escape his notice. He paused there to pray for the old monk he had come to find charming in barely the week's time that he had known him. The graveyard was peaceful, and he stood a long while in the cool, shaded space at the foot of James' grave, prayerfully remembering him and Peter and Gil Wetzel. He didn't know how long it was before he finally turned back toward the monastery.

His walk back up the hill toward his room was prayerful and pensive.

CHAPTER XXIV

When Raymond and John appeared at the abbot's door just before Noon Prayer, they both admitted to having nothing new, an admission that was, although disappointing, apparently not surprising to Abbot Mark.

"I keep hoping against hope that we'll have some sort of eureka moment to put our minds at ease. Please stay with this, both of you. And, by all means, get back to me the moment anything pops up," the abbot said, with an air of resignation.

Both promised to do so before going silently down the corridor with him to the Abbey church.

Father James' body arrived around 1:30, and word quickly got around the monastic community and school campus. All throughout the afternoon, monks drifted in and out of the church. University staffers made their way there, as well, to pay their respects to someone they had come to know and love.

Father John, for his part, put off going there until later in the afternoon, choosing, instead, to sit outside behind the monastery and take in the magnificence of Mount Rainier on the eastern horizon.

It was a quintessentially beautiful day in western Washington: the view of the mountain was completely unimpeded by clouds, and the air was pleasantly cool and dry. What Brother Michael had told him about the mountain flashed into his mind, that Indians had named it Tahoma, and that the name meant 'the mountain of God.' It looked so majestic in the distance and yet so peaceful. And for all its magnificence, he now realized, it was no more and no less awesome than people. He felt nestled in the love of God and gloried in it, and from the heart of that loving embrace, he prayed for Father James, Gilbert Wetzel and young Peter Hamilton. He even remembered to include Irene O'Carroll in Chicago and Annie Verden back in Algoma. All these people who had touched his life were in his prayers as he sat gazing at the mountain of God rising white and beautiful out of the Cascade Range to the east.

He sat for more than an hour before deciding to go into the church. Instead of going back through the building behind him, however, he walked out onto the monastery parking area to his left and followed the road upward to the church, the better to enjoy the beauty of the day for a few extra moments. That route took ten minutes, and he paid special attention to the magnificent greenery all around him during his stroll.

With all those of importance to him who had gone before him in his prayerful thoughts, he entered the hush of the Abbey church. Two monks were kneeling beside James' open casket. The monk's face was no longer contorted as Father John remembered it from the snack bar floor several days earlier. Having just spent an hour with James at the center of his prayers, he lingered only moments to gaze on his peaceful face and promised silently to return in the evening. He gave a blessing at the casket before turning to go back outside.

Back in the refreshing air outside the church entrance, Father John saw a middle-age monk making his way toward the church door. "Hello, Brother. I'm Father Wintermann. I don't think we've met before."

"No, we haven't. I'm Brother Nicanor. I teach Spanish here at our university."

The man didn't look to Father John particularly Hispanic. *Wonder how he got interested in Spanish?* "Good to meet you, Brother. You pronounce your name with a long 'a.'"

"Yes. I suppose you recognize it from the Acts of the Apostles."

"I do, but I also recognize it from the Mexican community back in my home diocese. Only, there it's pronounced with a short 'a.'"

"Interesting. But that would be entirely proper in Spanish, you see."

"And do they call you 'Nick' for short?"

"No. We had a Father Nicholas here, and he was often called 'Nick.' I suppose it made sense to call only one of us by that nickname."

He smiled. "Were you just in the church?"

"Yes. It's quiet. I was the only one there, except for two of your confreres kneeling by the casket. Olav was the only one that I recognized; the other I've not been introduced to. And I only just met Olav, actually. An interesting man, I must say!"

"Oh, he's our resident Republican — our *vocal* Republican, I mean. The monastery is just about split down the middle politically, but most of us don't speak about that very much. Olav's one of the few exceptions. Sometimes Theodosius joins him and, if they're successful, they can get Basil into an argument. He's the only somewhat vocal Democrat in the house. It's rare that any of his fellow

Democrats support him out loud. Most of us here in the monastery avoid that sort of thing. But that's not to say political passion isn't alive and well here. It's just that the majority of us don't relish even the appearance of disunity or dissension. Maybe, it's confrontation that we don't like."

"It wasn't politics that we were discussing, though," Father John said. "It had more to do with the younger monks. I guess they get under his skin occasionally."

"You're right. They do. But, strangely, he doesn't bring *those* feelings out into the open that often. He did with you, though, you say?"

"Yes. I can't even remember now how it came up, but it seemed to center on the youngsters being messier than he'd like."

"Oh, that! Well, he's not the only one who has that issue stuck in his craw. I think the abbot must hear about that from one or the other of us at least once a week. I rather think the situation is getting better, but it's a bone of contention around here, all right, and has been for quite a while. But then, if that's the only thing we have bothering us, I suppose we're not in such bad shape." He laughed a quiet little laugh, his face pinking from the effort.

"I haven't asked the abbot, but I'm guessing that I can vest for the funeral Mass and process in with you all?"

"I'm sure that you may. But you might want to talk to the abbot, just to learn what's different about our funerals here at the abbey."

"I'll do that, and thanks for the heads-up, Brother."

As the monk went into the church, Father John made a mental note to see the Abbot about the funeral, but he also decided that Nicanor didn't belong on any list of suspects. *If I were a betting man, I'd guess that that none of them really deserve to be on such a list.*

CHAPTER XXV

As Father John emerged from the dining room after supper, he stopped the abbot in the corridor to ask about the funeral. "May I vest tomorrow and process in with the monks at James' funeral Mass?"

"Certainly, Father. Stay in the middle of the line and just follow the lead of the monks ahead of you. Anything you find a little different shouldn't be hard to figure out and imitate, if you do that. And, by all means, please also walk with us to the cemetery. Has anyone told you where that is?"

"Yes. I've been there and prayed at James' grave, in fact. I was wondering, though: are the gravesites assigned, or can individual monks express a wish about where they'd like to be buried?"

"Oh, no. The next monk to die gets the next spot in the pattern. I'm not aware that any exceptions were ever made in our whole history here, not even for abbots."

"Sort of like at Gethsemani. Thomas Merton is buried next to the abbot — Abbot Fox, I believe — with whom he didn't get along very well. The monks there delight in pointing that out to visitors." Father John had a wry smile on his face.

The abbot smiled also. "Sauce for the goose … " he said, breaking away to talk with one of the monks who wanted his attention.

Father John spent the rest of that evening in his room, thinking about all the dead who were important to him in one way or another. He began with his family, gratefully remembering his parents and grandparents, calling especially to mind the many incidents that particularly endeared each of them to him.

He was also grateful that both of his siblings were still alive, and he made a quiet promise to contact them when he returned to Illinois. It had been, he decided, too long since they had spent time together. *The older I get, the more precious the people in my life become,* he thought.

He began to pick through his memory for those priests and religious he treasured. His aunt came immediately to mind: a nun, long dead now, but she had endeared herself to him for, among other things, the candy he always got from her desk drawer when he and his family visited her in his boyhood. He was sure that she had helped pray him into the priesthood, and he especially remembered how happy she was on the day of his ordination when he gave her his blessing.

Among the priests he thought of next were several teachers in the minor and major seminaries and, of course, the beloved pastor of his boyhood who was already an old man when he first knew him. But he chuckled to realize that the man had been far younger at that time than he was himself now.

How old is old when you're a kid? The man must have been in his forties then, and by the time I was ordained, he was probably in his mid- to late sixties ... not old by my standards now! Father Lawrence had almost certainly also helped his vocation with his prayers and example, he realized. *I should visit his grave in Maple Grove when I get back. Maybe my brother and sister will come along,* and we could visit the old homestead and those people in the Grove who still remember us.

There were also several members of his presbyterate in southern Illinois, priests whom he had long admired. *I don't think I've ever told those guys how I feel about them,* he realized with no little chagrin. *I'll* definitely *do something about that when I get back home. God knows it can be lonely ministering the way we priests do, without many people close to us and certainly with none at our beck and call to share with the way married people can! It certainly won't hurt to tell them how important they've been to me — and still are — and why I admire them so much. Hope I can do that without sounding maudlin.*

There weren't as many religious to whom he felt close, but one or two nuns who had taught or ministered at the parishes he'd been assigned to came to mind, as did one member of his minor-seminary class who had left to join the Jesuits. The two had stayed in touch off and on over the years, but Father John lost track of him five years earlier. The last he had heard, the man was in the Jesuit missions in New Guinea. Tracking him down became another priority on that long evening of prayerful recollection.

He did not attempt to make a list of all these people but relied, instead, on something like what his professor of moral theology had once said in class: semel pro semper — 'once for all time.' The priest had used the phrase to suggest that the seminarians make the determination at that very moment in class to consecrate *only* the bread that was on the corporal at all their Masses. Father John decided later that such thinking was entirely too mechanistic, and he determined to be very focused each time he celebrated the Eucharist, rather than relying on something like that.

He did something in his own prayer life, however, that was similar to the suggestion of his Benedictine teacher. He made categories for his prayerful remembrances and placed people and their intentions within those categories. He did not otherwise try to recall them individually later when at prayer. When he prayed, therefore, he would simply tell himself that he was praying for 'all the deceased in his family' or for 'those who have asked for my prayers.' It made praying easier and he never saw it as somehow a lesser way to pray.

That evening as he prayed and remembered, he said to himself, bemusedly, that perhaps he was doing the same thing after all. In any case, he was praying ... and praying for those who were special because they had touched his life and made him different — better — as a result.

He felt immensely thankful that night for all of those people, just as he felt grateful for Father James. He could only imagine how the people who knew and valued the elderly monk far better than he did must feel as they looked back at how the man had touched their lives. Knowing him for only a week, Father John felt nonetheless cheered by the man, eccentric though he had been, cheered by the simple joy the monk had shown in inviting him to pray with the entire community on the evening when they first spoke to one another. *I'll be glad to pray with the whole community again, James ... this time especially for you.*

He got to sleep quite late that night but made it to prayer with the monks on time in the morning.

CHAPTER XXVI

After breakfast Thursday, the whole monastery was abuzz with preparations for the funeral liturgy.

Father Julius, the Guest Master, was fussing over Father James' two relatives who, having arrived from Idaho late Wednesday evening, were staying at the Guesthouse across the road from the church. He had guided them through Morning Prayer, chaperoned them to breakfast and was now giving them a mini-tour of the main building before the funeral Mass.

Brother Jerome, the sacristan, was busy with last-minute adjustments to the flowers around the casket and altar, and several of the younger monks were listening intently to Father Jonathan in the sacristy, as he went over details concerning their serving at the funeral liturgy.

As he entered the cloister through the door nearest the church, Father John could hear the singers practicing in Father Justus' room nearby, and he felt fairly certain that the abbot was going over the words of his homily at the opposite end of the first floor.

He had stopped to peruse the bulletin board but found nothing new there and decided to pop back quickly into the church for a private prayer at the casket. That done, he was back at the bulletin board and still had more than an hour before vesting and joining the monks in the slype just before Mass. He was trying to figure out how to spend the remaining time, when Father William came around the corner to look at the bulletin board. It occurred to Father John to ask him about his responsibilities relative to the snack bar.

"Hello, Father William. All set for the funeral?"

"Yes. Poor James! I shall miss him. We were contemporaries here, you know. Friends for eons, it seems. We were here in the old days ... back when we were young. That was a vastly different time from today, but we shared some wonderful good times back then."

"I can imagine," Father John said. "I once asked an old man back in southern Illinois what the roads were like when he was young, and he told me that they were either dusty or muddy. He went on to say that unless you'd been there, you had no idea how slow that made traveling, even with the new-fangled cars."

"That sort of describes how we've changed here, too. I suppose you were told that this monastic foundation is more than one hundred years old. Well, James and I were here for most of that time, and unless you'd been here too, you probably can't fully appreciate how it was then.

"In the old days, the monks did a lot more of the work around here than is done now. We had a fully functioning farm, with horses and cows and chickens, and we did all the work to make it run. We did everything in the refectory too, from cooking to serving and cleaning up. We did have a lot more monks then, of course, so we had the manpower for those sorts of things. But, nonetheless, we did it all ... and took that for granted, too. There was no whining about it.

"James and I were often on the same work details. We cleaned out the barns together for several years. We took our turn working the kitchen — the scullery, as some of us called it then. We even went through the college here together; and we both taught in our high school.

"But when that closed, James and I got split up. He was originally from Idaho, and he went back there for parish work, whereas I upgraded my degree so I could teach here in our college. Those are precious memories to me, and I've been thinking about them a lot these past couple of days."

"I'll bet you have, Father. But if I may change the subject, I was wondering ... could you tell me more about your work in the snack bar? I only know that you're supposed to keep it clean, or something like that."

"That's about the size of it, all right. I look in from time to time during the day and straighten up whatever might need that. But, without fail, every night before I go to my cell after Night Prayer, I make one last stop to make sure everything's ship-shape in there."

"Ship-shape?"

"You know: clean any dirty dishes, put away whatever food might be left on the counter, check the refrigerator so everything's kosher in there ... see that nothing's spoiled and everything's properly capped and stored. Things like that!"

"Are there often dirty dishes? I'd think that the monks would police their own messes ... "

"From time to time there are, yes. Not often ... but once in a while I have to wash some dishes or utensils and put them away."

"Not often, you say? Are there repeat offenders or, as the phrase from 'Casablanca' goes: are there 'usual suspects'? Or is it, rather, pretty much random?"

"Well, yes, there are some regulars, I'm sorry to say. The young fellows, mostly! Sometimes I get after them. Other times I just tell the abbot that they're up to their old tricks. I guess he gets on their case ... I can't really be sure. It's more of a nuisance to me, rather than a real problem. But it does aggravate me at times, I have to admit."

"Was that the case when James died? Were there dirty dishes left about or other things to straighten up?"

"Not the day before he died. That night the place was just right when I looked in on it."

"And the day of his death ... ? What about the time *before* he died last Saturday?"

"I hadn't poked my head in there before our discovering poor James, so I haven't any answer for you about that."

"What about *right after he died*, then? Did you find anything that should have been put away? I mean, if you did, it would've been from sometime earlier that day, correct?"

"Raymond and I went back to the snack bar a few minutes after they removed James' body, and all we found were the knife that James had used to make his sandwich and the jelly jar. Both were on the counter. James was another of the usual suspects, as you put it. But none of us held that against him, what with his condition and all. I certainly never minded tidying up after him, I can tell you. Poor fellow!"

"Thanks, Father William. It's such a pity he had to go that way."

"I guess we haven't found out exactly how it all happened," Father William said softly, more to himself than to Father John.

Father John wondered how much William knew about the tangle that the abbot, Father Raymond and he were trying to sort through, but he decided not to get into that with the elderly monk standing there with him. Instead, he bade adieu and made his way back to his room.

By the time he had used the bathroom and gathered his wits together, it was time to make his way toward the church for the funeral.

CHAPTER XXVII

Father John donned his alb and white stole in the vesting room of the monastery and lined up silently with the Benedictines in the slype. As the opening hymn began, the line of monks began to move slowly forward into the church. From beginning to end, the ritual was one of celebration. There were no lugubrious moments or discordant notes, not even one suggestion that the abbey was doing anything that day other than glorying in a life well-spent by one of its own, all the monks at peace about their very own Father James having moved on to a fuller life and a well-deserved rest.

The church was far from full, but the assembly sang with enthusiasm, and the several monks standing near Father Justus at the organ handled the more specialized chants with lovely four-part harmony. The abbot's eulogy included several personal remembrances that were touching as well as humorous, and he spoke warmly about James' importance to the life and mission of the monastery.

Still, Father John's mind wandered occasionally throughout the Mass. All the dead who were so special to him kept vying with the liturgy for his attention. Having no designated role other than that of concelebrant, he found himself standing for a long time late in the ceremony, his mind on other things, despite the hymn that was being sung quietly during communion.

The moment presented a perfect opportunity for him to remember again the priests who had been important to him over the years. Suddenly, however, he realized that he had forgotten to include in his prayer any deacons he had known throughout his ministerial life. Feeling remiss, he began to call those men to mind. In their diaconal service, they had often performed yeoman duty on an entirely volunteer basis, sometimes putting the priests to shame with their selfless ministry.

There's Donald, of course, who was in the first parish at which I was pastor. What a help he was! And the doctor who treated me that time for poison ivy ... from Benton, or was it Harrisburg? The one with the terrible allergy that almost killed him one weekend during his diaconal training! What was it again? Oh, yes: eggs! He was extremely allergic to eggs and nearly died that Saturday night because ...

He looked up suddenly and wondered if his body had betrayed the fact that his mind had been elsewhere. Satisfied that no one had noticed any sudden movements that he might have made, he excitedly continued his internal monologue. *Of course! Why hadn't I thought of that before? The doctor almost died because of a tainted utensil. The fact that his wife was there and understood what was happening was the only thing that saved him. If she hadn't gotten him so quickly to the hospital in Belleville, the man would certainly have been gone. As it was, he got another ten years or better to serve with distinction as physician and deacon.*

This is important! I must *see Raymond. We absolutely have to rethink some things ...*

The service within the Abbey church was soon concluded, and the entire congregation moved outside in procession down the hill to the monks' cemetery. The slow walk plus the prayers at the grave consumed thirty minutes more, and with the return up the hill to the monastery plus more time spent taking off his vestments, it was close to an hour — an unnerving hour — before Father John was able to finally search out Father Raymond during the mass exodus from church to refectory. The abbot had invited everyone in attendance to eat with the monks afterward, and many from the service were making their way to the lowest floor of the main building as Father John sought out the Prior.

Given the horde of people at the food line, the two priests found it convenient to step aside and talk virtually unnoticed. It took a few minutes for Father John to explain to the Prior what he had in mind. When Raymond signaled his agreement, the two stepped through the dining room door at the other end of the room from where the cafeteria line was set up and made immediately for the abbot's table. While Father John discretely stood a few paces away, Father Raymond spoke briefly to the abbot in hushed tones. It was clear from his face that the abbot found Raymond's message of interest, and he soon whispered something back to the Prior.

Father John could barely contain himself as he stood waiting to hear what the abbot had said.

"He'll see us after the meal," Raymond reported. "Let's get into line. He can't very well break away from James' relatives right now, and we might as well eat."

"I'm anxious as all get out to follow up on this, but I think you're right. We can't do anything 'til the abbot breaks free." So Father John reluctantly joined the Prior at the tail end of the food line.

They both ate very little — and hastily, as well – but it took twenty-five minutes before the abbot became available. After his farewells to James' two cousins, he at long last signaled the two priests to follow him and cautioned them to withhold any discussion until they were in his quarters.

The walk to the monastery seemed interminable, but after Abbot Mark had finally closed the door to his office and offered them a seat, he spoke to Father John. "So, what's this idea of yours that Raymond alluded to in the dining room?"

"Perhaps I should first tell you what prompted it, Abbot," he replied. "I knew a doctor in southern Illinois who entered our deacon program. He was highly allergic to eggs and egg products. The training sessions were conducted at the Shrine the Oblates run outside Belleville and encompassed a whole weekend once each month. A priest friend taught Scripture in that program and was with them one weekend, and he told me what happened to the doctor at that training session.

"After the last class on Saturday night, most of the men and their wives invaded the kitchen — they had the run of the place, I gather — to make sandwiches before going to bed. To make a long story short, the doctor used a knife that had been used to spread mayonnaise on someone else's sandwich. It had been rinsed and wiped but not washed with soap, as it turned out. The residue from that mayo was enough to throw the man into shock almost instantly. Luckily, his wife knew what was happening, as well as what to do — she could even figure out later how the incident had been played out! She rushed him to the hospital and told the staff there what to do to save him. He did survive, even though he was very sick for some time afterward.

"When I remembered that, I got to thinking. Father Olav had complained to me about the young monks ... how, among other things, they weren't very tidy, especially in the snack bar. They don't clean up after themselves very well there, according to him." Remembering what Nicanor had told him about complaints coming regularly to the abbot, he kept watching the abbot's face carefully as he spoke, but didn't see a flicker of anything cross it.

"So I began to wonder if perhaps Brother Thomas may not have washed his knife after making his peanut butter sandwich the day James died ... may have just rinsed and wiped it and then left it there on the sideboard. If so, and if James used it to make his jelly sandwich ... "

"I see," Abbot Mark said. He sat with his forehead deeply wrinkled, pondering a long while before speaking again. Fathers John and Raymond sat expectantly, their eyes glued on him.

Before he could speak, however, Father John thought to add one more thing. "I asked Father William this morning about his responsibilities as to the snack bar, and he repeated what he'd said before, namely, that after James' death there was just one knife and the jelly jar on the counter. Now I figure that if Thomas says he didn't put his knife away after he used it — no matter what he did to clean it — it should mean that the knife James used was the same one Thomas had used. It only remains to find out what Thomas meant by saying that he had cleaned up after himself." Again, he looked expectantly at the abbot.

"Are you saying that the knife James used might have had traces of peanut stuff on it from Thomas' use of it — peanut oil ... whatever — and that was enough to do James in?"

"Precisely, Father Abbot," Father John said. "You said James was extremely allergic. That was the case with the deacon from my diocese, and look what happened to him. We've *got* to talk to Thomas again."

"I understand. But I still have one minor problem. I agree that we have to find out from Thomas exactly what he did in cleaning up that day. But, assuming the worst-case scenario, I don't want the end result to be such a huge guilt trip for Thomas that he might not get over it. Knowing him as I do, I worry that he might blame himself for James' death. We must avoid that at all costs. Whatever we do — whatever *you* do, Raymond — must be done so as to avoid that."

"Oh, I certainly agree, Father Abbot," the Prior said. "We must think this out carefully before I approach the young man. But I believe we *have to* approach him."

The three pondered that for what seemed to be at least a whole minute. Finally Father John ventured a thought. "What if you talk to him in a less formal way, Raymond. *Casually* bring the matter up. Mention the past history of the junior monks as occasionally being less than scrupulous, shall we say, in their policing of the snack bar ... and then ask if he's sure he put the peanut butter away. He'll say 'yes,' no doubt.

"Then, as though it were an after-thought, you can feed him a question about putting the knife back in the drawer. If you follow this procedure, no matter what he says, you mustn't look surprised or judgmental. Does this make sense so far?"

The two men nodded.

Father John continued. "This is the crucial part: you've got to find out if he washed the knife or not — washed it with soap, I mean. Perhaps you could say something like 'you washed it, didn't you, *or at least rinsed it off and wiped it dry?*' And again you've got to look noncommittal, no matter what he says. Maybe you could simply respond 'good' to *whatever* he says, implying that the matter is then finished. By the end of something like that, you should know whether there was a tainted knife left behind. And, with any luck, you won't have sown the seeds for any guilt feeling.

"And, to repeat, William said he found only one knife on the counter after James died — that and a jelly jar. In fact, if I remember correctly, he said you were with him, Raymond, when that determination was made. Correct?"

"Yes, I was there, and you've got it correct: a knife and the jelly jar were the only things left lying around there."

"So if Thomas left *his* knife behind, it's got to be the one that James used. To be determined, then, is whether it was washed or not." Father John paused for breath, and again there was silence.

After some thought, the abbot reached a decision. "That's what has to be done, then, Raymond. Can you search out Thomas and get this settled?"

But Father John immediately suggested caution. "It might be better to do it so that it looks like a chance encounter. Maybe you could see him at Haustus tonight, unless, of course, you *do* bump into him before then."

"I think that would be better, Abbot," Raymond agreed. "It shouldn't look anything other than casual … accidental."

"Let me know whenever you find out something definitive, then," the Abbot said, with a look in his eyes that Father John interpreted as hopeful. "But do it soon. The tension is threatening to get me down."

CHAPTER XXVIII

Father John went back to his room, his mind whirling. He was surprised at how eager he was feeling to discover exactly what Thomas had done that fateful day. But he knew that all he could do now was to wait out the process that had been set in motion.

He decided to pack most of his things for the next morning's flight. He would have just enough time in the morning for breakfast and the community Mass before heading to the airport for his departure at 11. Under the circumstances, it might just as well be now as later that day.

While the whole process didn't take very long, it did keep his mind off the business with Thomas, at least for the hour during which he fretted over his suitcase. Even repacking twice, which ultimately accomplished no noticeably better arrangement of his things, didn't use up nearly as much time as he wished.

He was of a mind to go next to the community room to read the newspapers there but thought better of it almost instantly. *What if I should run in Thomas?*

There was a TV room almost directly above him on the next floor. There might be something of interest on the tube. *And if I run into Thomas, I can always just leave, I suppose.*

Instead of using the stairs, he took the elevator and stepped into the room just a few feet away at the south end of the corridor. But daytime TV turned out to be boring, a mixture of soap operas, commercial channels hawking cheap jewelry and some reruns that hadn't even been funny or interesting when they were new. He soon gave up and walked back down to his room. *At least I didn't run into any monks.*

He was still faced with time on his hands and no way immediately evident to spend it. It was too late to call Algoma and check in with Betty at the parish. Shea's book didn't interest him at the moment. What to do?

He hadn't toured the conference facility on the far side of campus, nor had he seen the inside of the fine-arts building. But conference rooms didn't seem that interesting, and from what he knew of the other building, there were just practice rooms and an office or two there. Neither of those places seemed to promise any relief from his restlessness. As he didn't wish to bother the abbot, either, the only other thing that came to mind was a walk.

So he headed outside with no clear plan other than to stroll around the property. He hadn't gone very far — just past the Abbey church — when Father Julius came out of the Guesthouse and greeted him at a distance.

"Father, do you have a minute?" he called. "I was just asked to relay a message if I saw you. How fortuitous to find you almost immediately after that request!"

"What is it, Father Julius?"

"Brother Thomas helps me in the Guesthouse," he began. Father John felt a sinking feeling in the pit of his stomach.

"He's inside," Father Julius continued, "still putting the rooms in order that our visitors from Idaho had used. They've already left, if you didn't know. Anyway, Brother Thomas would like to see you. He heard that you were leaving tomorrow, and I suppose he wants to say goodbye. I told him that whatever he wanted, it could probably wait 'til supper, but he was insistent. He said that he would also go looking for you himself, if I didn't find you. But on the slim chance that I could reach you first, he ... Well, you understand. He's inside here. Let me get the door for you. There's a separate code for the Guesthouse — you can understand why, no doubt."

He had turned back toward the Guesthouse almost immediately upon beginning to speak to Father John and had by this time reached the facility's front door. He had it open quickly, continuing to speak all the while. "There. Now you can get in. Just call out to Thomas, he'll answer. He's the only one in there right now."

"Thanks, Father."

"Glad to help," the Guest Master said and held the door for Father John before heading back toward the monastery.

Father John's mind was racing. *Has Raymond gotten to him already? Does he want to talk to me ... about* murder? *Good Lord, what am I into now?*

He tentatively called Thomas' name.

The young monk responded immediately from the other end of the building and shortly afterward popped his head out of one of the far rooms. "That was quick! Do you mind, Father? I'd like to talk to you. It shouldn't take long. At least, I hope it won't. Just let me finish this room, however. Give me several minutes."

Father John continued to recycle the direst of thoughts as he fidgeted by the door. When Thomas reappeared with an armload of dirty linen, Father John finally took several steps in his direction.

"Is this where I would have stayed had I been a layman wanting a retreat at your monastery?" He was trying to sound casual.

"Yes, it is. Let me just put these sheets in here ... " He stepped into a room and reappeared instantly. "Now I'm freed up. Is it okay, Father? I'd like to go to confession. And we can do it here. There's no one around. Should have all the privacy we need."

Father John's worst fears appeared to have been realized. He tried to look calm as he agreed to the request. "Where exactly, then?"

"This room should work. There are comfortable chairs in here." The young man was indicating what seemed to be a sitting room or lounge.

"Fine." But the word hardly fit Father John's emotional state.

As they entered the room, the young monk glanced at his watch and, with a pained look, said: "Oh, my gosh. I forgot. I promised Justin some help with his French. He's boning up for a class this fall with Brother Hilary. It's a second-level course, and he feels his French is rusty enough to require prepping. So I've been helping him all summer. Today's another of those tutoring moments, and I'm already late! I feel so sorry and *so embarrassed* about this, Father."

"I understand," Father John said, trying not to betray how relieved he actually felt.

But both the look on the young man's face and his tone of voice did not indicate anything like the gravity or the urgency that the priest had anticipated, and his relief quickly gave way to confusion.

"Don't misunderstand, Father. I *really* do want to go to confession. And I'd rather it be with you than ... " His voice trailed off.

" ... one of your confreres?" Father John tried not to sound patronizing as he completed the young man's sentence.

"Yes," he said, simply, his face reddening.

"I understand that sort of thing completely, son," Father John said, his sympathy suddenly triggered. "Not to worry. We can do it another time." *Or, if I'm lucky, not at all!* But he was instantly ashamed of that thought and tried not to betray that to the young monk.

Thomas' face reddened even more now that his reticence had been detected. "Well, I know you're to be leaving soon," he said, "and I don't want to miss the opportunity ... " Again, his voice trailed off.

"Yes, I leave tomorrow right after Mass."

"So, can we still do this? Tonight? After supper, maybe?"

"I'm sure we can." The relief that he had felt was already proving short-lived, but he was thankful for even such a small respite. *At least I'll have some time to think. Not everything here is making sense ... not by a long shot!*

"Oh, thank you," Thomas said, gratitude clearly evident on his face.

"My room, perhaps? I'm just across from the abbot."

"I know. That is, I know where that room is. I'll see you there after supper, then. But one more favor, please. Would you mind very much if we arrived there separately?" Another tinge of red was beginning to show on his face.

"Not at all. If you beat me there, just wait. I'll be along."

They left it at that. The monk broke away at a brisk pace and was out the door in seconds and on his way to the monastery, while Father John was left standing there, pondering too many new possibilities.

CHAPTER XXIX

He stepped outside and, with no other options evident to him, decided to continue his walk. He tried to keep his gait leisurely and his face calm, but his thoughts were a blur ... his many thoughts ... his far-too-many thoughts! *Slow this down, John. Take it easy. One thing at a time, if you please!*

Thomas wants to go to confession ... and not to a monk. That's ominous ... at least on the face of it. But could it mean anything else?

Nothing came to him.

Move on! Did Raymond get to him yet? He must have. Why else this confession business? It couldn't merely be a simple, straightforward request on Thomas' part, could it? He simply wants to receive the sacrament? I wouldn't think so. But what else, then, could it be? Some secret failing, something that at least he *thinks of as shameful? Not likely,* Father John decided, after juggling the probabilities.

He was deep in these thoughts when he glanced over his shoulder and saw the Prior uphill on the road behind him, apparently having just come from the lower floor of the Guesthouse. *Alumni and financial offices are down there, I think. Why would he go there, I wonder? No matter. Can I get his attention without arousing any suspicion? It's worth a try!*

"Father Prior," he said, loudly but not quite shouting. The monk kept walking.

"Father Raymond," he called out again, much louder now. This time the Prior turned toward him.

"May I have a word with you?" He had already started to walk in the man's direction, the better to be able to talk softer.

Raymond held up his left arm and pointed to his watch, as if to indicate that he was perhaps late for something important. "Can it wait?" he shouted back.

"I suppose so," Father John said and stopped, dejectedly.

"See you after Evening Prayer," the Prior said and hurried on his way toward the monastery.

Doesn't seem to be my day, or at least not my hour! You'd think that Raymond would have told me right away if he had seen Thomas. So perhaps that hasn't happened yet. That makes little sense, however, given what Thomas seems up to!

On the other hand, maybe he has *seen the young man but his first allegiance is to the abbot. That could explain his haste to get into the monastery. It's a very good possibility, I must admit.*

But if that is the case, I could go to the abbot right now ... He thought better of that almost instantly, however. *It is, after all, not really my business, is it? I will be told in due time, I'm sure.*

It's just that anything Raymond discovers will likely have a bearing on that confession. I must corner him at Haustus. He doesn't need to know about the confession, but I need to know if he's found out anything!

He abruptly stopped walking and began to chastise himself. *What do you mean, John? You're not a judge or jury. That kind of thinking about the sacrament of reconciliation went out with the Council. You'll be nothing but the soul of compassion with Thomas, no matter what Raymond says or doesn't say! Get your mind right!*

The remainder of the walk to his room became an extended act of contrition, and he continued praying until the bell for Evening Prayer.

CHAPTER XXX

Despite his desperate curiosity to learn what Raymond knew, Father John corralled his wayward thoughts and spent a generally prayerful twenty-five minutes with the monks in the chapel. He forced himself to rein in his emotions throughout Evening Prayer, making only one concession to them by rising immediately at the prayer's end and making his way to the lobby, the better to flag down the abbot and Prior relatively unobtrusively as they emerged at the head of the formal recessional.

The abbot signaled the two to follow, and they all made their way wordlessly to his quarters. Only once they were inside with the door closed behind them, did the abbot break the silence.

"Raymond, have you found out anything yet?"

He hasn't told the abbot! That must mean he hasn't seen Thomas yet! Hoping desperately that was somehow not the case — since nothing else could explain to Father John Thomas' request for confession — Father John waited nervously for the Prior's answer.

"I'm sorry I couldn't get to you before now, Abbot, but I was waylaid this afternoon by the school finance people. They had questions about the proposal the Abbey Council put forward for helping to fund the new campus building. I had to find our treasurer, Brother Jovian, to get some clarifications, and I was with him most of the afternoon."

"So then, you haven't seen Thomas yet?"

"On the contrary, I have."

Father John silently breathed a sigh of relief.

"It was a felicitous chance encounter before that money business. I got all the information we need, and I got it in very casual fashion."

"And ... ?" The abbot was exhibiting more impatience than Father John felt.

"It was more or less as you suspected, Father John. The young man told me that he had cleaned the knife but left it on the sideboard."

"And by 'cleaned,' he meant what, Raymond?" the abbot asked, impatience now even more clearly evident in his voice.

"You were right, Father John," the Prior said, looking pointedly and with obvious admiration at Father Wintermann. "All he did was rinse the blade, wipe it dry and leave it on the counter, though I'm sure he thought he'd done everything that was necessary and proper."

The three men stood looking at one another.

"And Thomas?" The abbot finally asked. "Did he suspect what you discovered ... what it means, that is?" The abbot's tone of voice switched from impatience to concern for his young charge.

"I don't believe so," Raymond said, drawing his words out slowly.

"But I should keep a close watch on him? Is that what you're implying, Raymond?"

"It wouldn't hurt. Guilt can be so damaging, as you implied."

Father John's mind was racing. *Do I mention Thomas' request for confession? That's a no-brainer, John: of course not! It's all tied to the seal of confession. Thomas has rights, after all. You don't even know what he's going to say, for that matter; and you couldn't tell, even if you did. Forget it! Forget it! Forget it!*

He smiled at Raymond, and with as much grace as he could muster, shrugged off the implied compliment from moments earlier. "Thanks for your kind words. It's just my peculiar kind of luck, and it's either a blessing or a curse, depending on how you look at it," he said, smiling.

"Well that settles it, then," the abbot said, looking like a huge burden had just fallen from his shoulders. "I'm glad we finally got to the bottom of it. Thank you, especially, Father John. It was, as I think you said the other day, an unfortunate accident, after all."

"Somewhere down the pike," he said, now looking at the Prior, "we'll have to refine the rules for the snack bar, Raymond. But I think we'll let several weeks go by before we do. That'll also give us time, you and me both, to carefully observe young Thomas."

"Supper will taste especially good tonight," Raymond said.

"Which sounds like a hint to allow talking tonight. I think we can do that, and we'll do it in honor of your last evening among us, Father John. That's occasion enough, so far as I'm concerned," the abbot said, glancing at both men with a broad smile on his face. "After all, the abbot should have a few perks," he said, winking at the abbey's guest.

"So be it, then," Raymond said. "Shall we go directly to the dining room? The bell will be sounding in a few moments."

After the appropriate announcement and explanation several minutes later at the doorway of the refectory, Father John led everyone inside, and the room was soon filled with the babble of small talk.

Father John was invited to the abbot's table for his last evening at St. Martin's, and Abbot Mark carefully kept the conversation light and virtually centered upon their guest.

The only time he had to himself came when he went back to the steam table for seconds on the vegetables, and the brevity of the moment didn't allow for much else than the realization that the upcoming confession would likely require a sizable dose of help from the Holy Spirit.

Deep within himself, Father John feared that Thomas hadn't told Father Raymond quite exactly what he'd done. *Either that or the young man knew something that he didn't feel comfortable telling the Prior, maybe even something about a third party.* Father John didn't like the possibilities but knew that all too soon it would all become clear.

On the walk back to the monastery after supper, Father John was paired with Brother Anselm, a normally reticent older monk. But that evening the man was full of conversation. Talking during the meal had perhaps loosened his tongue, was all Father John could make of it.

He inquired about all the standard things: what his ministry was like, was he planning to retire, what the weather was like in Illinois.

"Southern Illinois," Father John gently corrected him. "Elsewhere in our state, summers *can occasionally* be tolerable, but down our way it's a rare day that the temperature and humidity don't hover near triple digits."

"That bad?"

"I kid you not. Good for crops, but hard on lots of people, especially any who are built like me." He grinned.

"Hot dang," the monk said. "Our weather out here probably just tickles you to death!"

"Hot dang?"

"Yes. Why?"

"You could come from our neck of the woods if that's a favorite expression of yours."

"It's a favorite in my home area, too. I hail from southeastern Oregon. I guess I never lost a bunch of things I inherited back there." He smiled, and it was the first time Father John had seen him do so during his stay at St. Martin's. *Smiles* and *conversation! I like it!*

"You're right, I must say, about your weather here," Father John said. "I'd like to bottle it and take it back with me. While I can truthfully tell you it'll feel good to get back, I'll also admit that it's not the weather that's enticing me. It's my people at St. Helena's!"

It took Father John another several minutes at the abbot's entrance before he was able to bid farewell to the monk, so voluble had the man proven to be that evening.

When he finally rounded the corner inside, no one was standing outside his door. *I don't know how I beat him, but I hope Thomas will be along soon.*

He went inside his room but left the door slightly ajar for his penitent.

CHAPTER XXXI

Another five minutes went by before the young man appeared. He stepped quietly into the room and closed the door just as quietly. He sat down in the easy chair and faced Father John, who was seated at the room's small desk, then immediately began to speak in a near whisper: "Bless me, Father, for I have sinned … "

Father John interrupted. "Pardon me, Thomas, but let's approach this more gently, if you don't mind. After all, you said it probably wouldn't take long, so we should have enough time for a kinder pace.

"To begin with, tell me about yourself, since I really don't know you. And I can also tell you something about myself."

That seemed to throw the young man off balance. He paused momentarily, as though gathering his thoughts, then said: "But I just want to make a confession, Father."

"I know, Thomas, but the sacrament isn't something magical, as though all you do is say one incantation and I respond with another and then the magic happens. It's a human interaction. If I'm to pardon you in the name of the church, in the name of the people of God, we need to go about this in a more personable fashion. So why don't we get to know each other, at least a little bit? Perhaps I should start.

"I'm in my mid-sixties and have been a priest in parish work for going on forty years. I grew up in and minister in southern Illinois, and the Benedictines at St. Meinrad Seminary are largely responsible for my being the kind of priest I am. I really like parish work and I really love my people.

"There. I hope that gives you a small peek into my life. But feel free to ask for more, if need be, to get a better sense of who this confessor of yours is. After that, you can tell me a bit about yourself."

The young monk sat speechless, in all probability confronted with a perspective on sacramental reconciliation that was utterly new to him. When he finally spoke, he began to respond slowly to Father John's invitation.

"I am twenty-two years old, Father, and I entered the monastery after being so impressed with the monks that I came to know here as a student."

Father John wondered instantly if Thomas weren't the one who left the patio door open on the first morning of his retreat, but he quickly turned his attention back to the young man's words.

"I've been here two years and have been considering priesthood. But the final decision on things like that is up to the Abbey Council, and nothing will be done for another year or more, at any rate. They'll wait at least until I make final vows, and who knows if I'll still be of a mind for seminary studies then!

"I'm from Centralia, which is not far south of here, and I'm the oldest of three kids.

"Is that the sort of thing you're looking for, Father?"

"That's very helpful. But can you also tell me about how you fit in at the monastery?" Father John didn't know what prompted that question, but he was in hopes that it might somehow help flesh out the picture of this young man.

"Fit in? Are you asking about what I do here or how I like it here or how the others accept me here?"

"Wow! I hadn't thought far enough ahead to realize it could tell us all those things. Give me whatever seems right to you." *That was a better question than I realized, I guess!*

"Well, I do lots of manual labor here in the abbey, like the other junior monks, and when the Novice Master isn't available to supervise us, I'm often put in charge of the work detail. As far as liking it here, I certainly do. It was definitely the right decision to enter St. Martin's. And I like the monks I live with, and with few exceptions, I think they like me. Those of us my age are really close. We get along well, even though as individuals we have diverse tastes in politics, music and things like that."

He stopped, as though he were thinking about what to add, but then looked up to say: "I guess that's about it."

"Thanks, Brother. Just one final thing: please tell me what your thinking is about the sacrament of reconciliation."

That seemed to stump the young man, so Father John continued.

"What I'm looking for, Brother, is whether you see it as a call to change or a quick fix for problems and failings?"

"I know it's supposed to help change your life, Father, but I don't see that happening much with me, to be honest."

"Good. I mean that it's good you see the need for change as essential to the sacrament. As to that not happening as much or as fast as you'd like, welcome to the club!"

He paused. "I think we can begin now. Let us pray."

He offered a spontaneous prayer before inviting Thomas to join him in the Our Father. Then he said gently: "Please tell me what's troubling you."

This time, Thomas didn't repeat the stock formula he had used earlier but, instead, simply said, "I thought I had always gotten along with the establishment here ... you know: the abbot, the Prior, my Novice Master. But today the Prior quizzed me again about James' death ... "

Here it comes. I was afraid of this. Father John struggled not to betray his fears by any change in his body language.

" ... and I think that he doesn't trust me, or maybe doesn't believe me. I fear I've upset him and, though I've racked my brain, I can't imagine what I did or didn't do that would turn him against me like that."

Or maybe here it doesn't *come! This isn't going where I expected it would.* "What *exactly* did he ask you, Thomas? You *may* be making too much of what could be a little thing."

"I don't remember his exact words, but he asked about what I did after fixing my sandwich — did I put things away. I've told him that stuff twice already, and here he was asking again."

"He pulled you aside and quizzed you, you're saying?"

"Not exactly ... he bumped into me — in the snack bar, of all places — and brought it up. He said something about that room reminding him of James and his death. Then he said something like: 'you *did* put the peanut butter away' and 'you *did* clean the knife?'"

"And what did you say?"

"I told him yes. I told him I did both things."

"And did that satisfy him?"

"I'm not sure, but he didn't pursue the matter any further."

"Did he leave then or keep talking or what?"

"He stuck around and made small talk about one or two of the projects that we were involved in. Lately the junior monks have been working in our forest, cleaning up fallen trees and hauling the wood back for use in the stove at our lodge on Puget Sound."

"It seems to me, Brother, that if he stayed to talk about such things, your conclusion about his not liking you is a pretty big stretch. There could be a host of things going on there. For one, have you considered what kind of stress James' death might have caused him? If not exactly a contemporary of his, James is certainly someone Raymond could have looked up to. I wouldn't think it odd that his death be on the Prior's mind these days, or even for some days to come, for that matter.

"Pardon me if I hazard a guess here — and please correct me if I'm off base. I'm thinking that you may not be completely at home in your own skin yet. To put it another way: Do you like yourself?" He paused. "Why I ask is one sign that a person is not very secure is the need for approval."

Brother Thomas had been listening intently to Father John and, as the priest finished, the blush on the young man's face gave him away, even before he could acknowledge the accuracy of the priest's suspicion.

"Is it that obvious?"

"Let's not make too big a thing of this, son. There's no need to feel embarrassed. We can talk about that issue momentarily.

"First, however, let me get something clear in my own mind. You're here for confession, but I don't see anything *sinful* in what you've been saying so far. Did I mislead you as we began? I recall asking 'what's bothering you.' That may not have been clear to you, but I was hoping it would lead you into a confession of sin. Instead, what I've heard were things that indeed bother you but aren't sinful. Help me out here ... "

"Isn't displeasing your religious superiors sinful, Father?" His face indicated that he was utterly serious.

"I don't know what your Novice Master or spiritual director may be telling you, but I can say what I think. The answer to your question is, in a word, no. I don't see how it's your job to please people here, not even — or *especially* — the big shots. Your job is more or less the same as monk and Christian: you are to act lovingly to everyone in your life.

"If you think about it, you can control that. What you can't control is how others respond. You can't control whether anyone *likes* you. And since both sin and virtue involve things over which one has control, what you mentioned just now doesn't seem sinful at all. Am I being clear?"

Dawning recognition was beginning to glint in the eyes of the young penitent, and he began to speak hesitantly. "I guess that community has meant to me that we all have to get along, and since I'm one of the new guys here, I figured I have to bend over backward to make sure I fit it in."

"There's some truth in that, but 'getting along' doesn't mean being exactly like your confreres or espousing their opinions, especially to have them like you. And they certainly don't have to like *everything* about you, either. When you mentioned the junior monks earlier, didn't you note that you're all different in numerous ways?"

"Yes ... "

"But you like each other, right? You said so."

"I did. And it's true. We get along great."

"Then, as far as Father Raymond goes, the both of you don't have to hold the same views or even don't have to find each other as appealing as you happen to find your contemporaries. It's just a fact of life that we all differ and are attracted by different things and in different ways. Nothing to feel guilty about that sort of thing! How can there possibly be any blame assigned for that?"

"I think I see your point ... "

"Good. But, for all that, there's even less to worry about in your case. According to what you said, it's not even a question of Raymond disagreeing with you, let alone disliking you. Nothing you said told me that Raymond was showing disapproval. That you saw it otherwise tells me you're probably unsure of yourself and think that only literal and unambiguous approval from your superiors will help you feel okay. Raymond didn't disapprove, and you don't need his approval anyhow — not in that way! Maybe that's the simplest way to put it."

Thomas sat, digesting what his confessor had been saying.

Father John sat nervously waiting for another shoe to drop. *Please, Lord, no 'M' word!*

"I think I feel better, Father." Thomas had looked up with a broad smile on his face.

"That's nice to hear, Brother. Perhaps you'd like to finish your confession, then."

"There really isn't anything else, Father. Could I just say that I'm sorry for all the sins of my past life?"

Father John couldn't believe what he was hearing. *No 'M' word! Thomas hasn't made the connection the abbot was so worried about.*

"Certainly," he said, "and I'll be glad to assign you a penance."

After the absolution, they said a final prayer together, but before Thomas could stand to leave, Father John touched his arm gently to detain him momentarily.

"In the light of our conversation, Thomas, it might not be a bad idea for you to have a talk with Father Raymond." Father John was searching for some way to alert the powers that be not to worry about a guilt trip from their young charge. "It could be helpful for you both."

"Do you really think so?" Thomas' face was showing some concern.

"I see some merit in the idea, yes," Father John replied. "But if you don't feel up to that, maybe I could help. It's just that religious superiors want to promote harmony in their houses, and speaking with Raymond might help him avert any future misunderstandings with newcomers."

"That sounds like a good thing. But how could *you* help?"

"Well, you would have to give me permission to discuss the gist of what we talked about here. I promise not to say anything that might embarrass you. I have in mind letting Father Raymond know that junior monks might understand the intricacies of community just a little differently than their elders. For all I know, it could lead to their tweaking how they train you."

"Nothing embarrassing?"

"Certainly not. I'll go out of my way to avoid that."

"Well, if you think it might help the monastery … "

"No guarantees, Brother, but how can it hurt?"

"Okay, then." His face had lost its look of concern.

"To be precise, now: I have your permission to speak without fear of violating any of your rights or breaking the seal of confession?"

"You do, Father. And thank you for caring like that."

Father John gave Thomas his blessing and, after the young man had left, sat down in the recently vacated easy chair to count his blessings.

I can see Raymond and the abbot after Night Prayer. Who would have thought it? Everything's fallen into place. Thank You, Holy Spirit!

CHAPTER XXXII

He was able to step across the hall en route to Night Prayer in the Abbey church and alert the abbot about needing to see him and Raymond afterward and, twenty-five minutes later, the trio was seated in the abbot's office.

"I have Brother Thomas' permission to relay the essence of the confession he made after supper tonight. I don't think, first of all, that you have to worry about any guilt trip. From what he said to me, he's clearly unaware that his actions were in any way connected to James' death."

"Thanks be to God," Father Raymond said softly.

"I agree. Secondly, however, he was worried that he had offended you, Raymond, and that you didn't believe or trust him."

"Why, that's not even remotely accurate," the Prior quickly said.

"Oh, I know. But, you see, it points to something that you may need to be aware of. Young guys like him may well see community in this religious setting as involving the pleasing of their superiors. And they might require obvious approval, perhaps even in virtually all things, as a sign that they've done that. They could be more insecure, I guess I'm saying, than you might notice."

The abbot, who had been sitting in silent observation, finally spoke up. "That may be just another side of what I wanted to watch for in Thomas. Someone more mature wouldn't bear such watchfulness. Such a person wouldn't entertain doubts or feel guilt under these circumstances. What you've brought to our attention,

Father, is just another ramification of the immaturity in a number of young applicants to monasteries like ours. I'm glad that we may not have to shepherd Thomas through some guilt trip — that would be far trickier than what you've warned us about. But helping him navigate through the minefields of insecurity won't necessarily be a piece of cake, either. Thank you for the heads-up."

"Glad I could assist, Abbot. I had initially suggested that Thomas have a conversation with you about that, Raymond, but he didn't seem to favor that idea. It was then that I suggested I could grease the skids by relaying the message myself. But I want to be sure again that you've heard me: I got his permission to share the heart of what he said. You got the bonus of a conclusion of mine, too. But I did get his permission!"

"I — we — understand," Abbot Mark said and glanced at Raymond, who was nodding in return.

"I'm skittish about that," Father John said, "in large part because what brought me here involved my facing that very issue. Twice for that kind of thing in one summer is quite enough, thank you!" He smiled nervously.

"I can only imagine," the abbot said.

"Oh, yes, there's one more thing. I promised that I wouldn't say anything to you embarrassing to young Thomas. I think — I hope — I've avoided that. More to the point, he seems to be very sensitive about his felt need for approval. Best you should both be aware of that."

"Thank you again, Father. Before we conclude tonight, however, let me say that it has been a joy having you with us this week, Father John — quite aside from your help with our excitement here during your stay. May Father Raymond and I give you a blessing as you prepare to depart?"

"Yes. May I also have the blessing for travelers?"

CHAPTER XXXIII

The next morning, his last moments at St. Martin's went by very quickly. Before he knew it, the morning Mass was over and he was hauling his suitcase and carry-on bag to the elevator. Brother Michael was already there in the monks' parking area when he stepped out the far door on the lowest level of the monastery, and they were off to SeaTac Airport several minutes before 9.

Michael said that they should make good time because the morning rush hour was nearly over. He expected that it would take forty minutes to reach the airport. "And security at SeaTac has been fairly fast lately, so there should be no problem making your flight, Father. That's why Abbot Mark suggested you'd have time for Mass this morning."

The drive north on I-5 went by in no time, and they arrived at American Airlines at 9:45. Father John thanked his driver once again for introducing him to Mt. Rainier and waved goodbye from curbside check-in. He arrived at his gate well before boarding began.

Only when he was able to plop down into his aisle seat on the plane did he take time to slow down and begin the process of thinking back over his time with the Benedictines at St. Martin's.

He wondered what it meant that strange and mysterious things had been popping up at nearly every turn of late. *It certainly makes life interesting!*

Looking forward to returning to Algoma, as he did, he found himself hoping that there wouldn't be anything strange and mysterious awaiting him there. *I think I can do with a little peace and quiet right now, and I imagine my cat-lickers at St. Helena's can, too.*

Though the Shea volume was in his carry-on, he was content to meditate for a while before cracking it open to review what it had to say about the next Sunday's gospel selection.

Father Peter had been a singular grace.

Looking back on everything, it was pretty audacious of me to think so poorly of You, Lord. But I suppose that each one of us has to work through a fair share of ignorance and shortsightedness before being able to arrive at the insights that alone can give us peace. It's laughable, in retrospect, that I could see that process as normal for my spiritual charges but think that I should not need it. Thanks for putting me in my place. Anyway, I think I want to stay in touch with that wise old monk who helped me so gently and so well. If nothing else, he may be a great resource when someone brings me a problem that stumps me.

He tilted his seat back as far as it would go, intending to relax and perhaps even nap, but his mind kept dwelling on the Holy Spirit. It occurred to him that the Holy Spirit had been at work in bringing him to St. Martin's and in the abbot's choice of Father Peter. And he was well aware of his debt of gratitude for the Spirit's assistance with Brother Thomas. In the midst of thanking the Holy Spirit for all that, he had a sudden realization.

The Spirit had been far more active than that. He began to see a spiritual thread connecting everything as far back as Annie Verden, if not beyond.

As he thought back over the events of the past year, he was more and more convinced that it had been the Spirit that helped him bring healing to Annie and the people in her life. And it had to be the Spirit that brought him to Chicago last Christmas and worked though him to help Michael and Irene. And it certainly had to be divine help that helped him to reach out to Gilbert Wetzel and the families of those young fellows in Algoma recently.

Come to think of it, the Spirit probably began preparing me for these strange and mysterious things as far back as Annie's death, seeing ways that I could never dream of for bringing healing and spiritual growth to people even in the midst of sorrow and apparent tragedy.

How beautiful!

And how grateful I am to have been chosen for that.

And now to have brought me to Washington, not only for my own spiritual growth, but also to allow me to be of help, first to Robert and then to the whole abbey! It's amazing that You reminded me of that deacon, Lord, and then used that to bring peace of mind to the monks.

And, of course, it was Your assistance when I needed it during Thomas' confession. Thank You! Thank You, Lord!

With the hint of a smile on his lips, he settled back at last for a nap. But the word 'Thomas' kept moving in and out of his mind. Then he realized why.

It was for Brother Thomas, after all, that he was brought to St. Martin's!

Thomas was far more important than the mystery surrounding Father James, more important than Brother Robert's fall, more important even than his own spiritual dilemma. It was Thomas, all along! And the Holy Spirit was behind it all. He was convinced of that now; in a flash it had all become clear.

It's like honing one's skills as a baseball player, he decided. *You go through all the physical drills and mentally reinforce them. Pitchers learn to defend against the sacrifice bunt by repeatedly snaring the ball and flicking it to first. Repetition after physical repetition: snare and flick, snare and flick. And then you reinforce that by visualizing the play and repeating to yourself over and over again: snare and flick, snare and flick.*

But when the situation comes in a real game, the circumstances might shift ever so slightly. There's a bunt, all right, but it's a suicide squeeze, and you have only a second to realize that the snare-and-flick must be aimed at home, not first. If you're good, if you're a real pro, it works. And you know, later, that all your training was a good thing, but you also know that, in that one instance, it was a hard-to-define something else that actually helped you make the play.

Father John knew that his hard-to-define something was the Holy Spirit.

For all his certainty that his training would take care of every pastoral instance he may ever be confronted with, there was, in fact, that occasional instance when he would get his comeuppance and have to face that fact that the Spirit is in charge. Always!

Amazing!

And it was Thomas all along! Amazing!
Thomas!
Amazing!

FATHER JACK FRERKER'S BOOKS

During a long hot summer (<u>HEAT</u>) in the fictional town of Algoma, a place where everyone knows everything about everyone, there is nonetheless a mysterious death which Father John Wintermann helps solve and brings spiritual healing to those affected by it.

The following Christmas, in Chicago for a funeral (<u>SOLSTICE</u>), the priest explains yet another death and helps those close to the deceased find peace.

The next spring (<u>CONSPIRACY</u>), drug related crimes and deaths threaten the peacefulness of Algoma. Father John helps to end the turmoil and is instrumental in the conversion of the perpetrator.

By mid-summer, Father John is in search of his own peace of mind at an abbey in Washington, where more mysteries await him—and grace as well (<u>MONKSBANE</u>).

The relationship between a priest and his bishop over three decades (<u>CONNECTIONS</u>) highlights the importance of human ties, especially in the lives of priests.

The books and the audio version of <u>MONSKBANE</u>, can be gotten from Father Jack through his web page (www.paxpublications.com) or by mail to 7710 56th Avenue NE, Olympia WA 98516.

To order copies of **MONKSBANE** please fill out the order form below, tear it out and enclose it + your check in an envelope addressed to:

PAX Publications

7710 56th Avenue NE

Olympia WA 98516

Please specify **PRINT VERSION** or **AUDIO VERSION**

Inquiries may be sent to the above address or to: jackfrerk@aol.com

---

ORDER FORM

Please ship _____ copies of **MONKSBANE** by Jack Frerker

Retail price (**BOOK**): $15.00 (plus $4.00 per copy Shipping/Handling)

Retail price (**AUDIO**): $20.00 (plus $4.00 per copy Shipping/Handling)

Phone: _____ E-mail: _____

Make checks payable to: PAX PUBLICATIONS

Payment of $_____ is enclosed

Signature _____

Shipping Information:

Name: _____

Address: _____

City: _____

State: _____ Zip: _____